On 1984

Quotes for the Orwellian Future
Happening Today

EDITED BY JAMES DALEY

Racehorse Publishing

Racehorse Publishing books may be purchased in bulk at special discounts for sales promotion, corporate gifts, fund-raising, or educational purposes. Special editions can also be created to specifications. For details, contact the Special Sales Department, Skyhorse Publishing, 307 West 36th Street, 11th Floor, New York, NY 10018 or info@skyhorsepublishing.com.

Racehorse Publishing™ is a pending trademark of Skyhorse Publishing, Inc.®, a Delaware corporation.

Visit our website at www.skyhorsepublishing.com.

10 9 8 7 6 5 4 3 2 1

Library of Congress Cataloging-in-Publication Data
is available on file.

Jacket artwork: iStockphoto

ISBN: 978-1-63158-221-9
eISBN: 978-1-63158-222-6

Printed in the United States of America

Table of Contents

Introduction 1

Fake News and Alternative Facts
(Or, Quotations on Propaganda, Lies,
and Freedom of the Press) 7

Bad Hombres
(Or, Quotations on the Nature of Fear and Prejudice) 35

Draining the Swamp
(Or, Quotations on Politics and Corruption) 65

Order and Strength
(Or, Quotations on Fascism, Oppression, and Tyranny) 85

Resistance 113

Introduction

When George Orwell sat down to write his anti-authoritarian classic, *1984*, just shy of two years after the end of WWII, there was a feeling throughout many of the free nations of the world that fascism and autocracy had been roundly defeated, once and for all. Even in the mid-1930s, long before the U. S. or Britain had entered into the war, there was a common belief in both nations that they were immune to the type of tyranny they saw taking place in Germany, Italy, Russia, and elsewhere. In fact, this belief was so widespread, that in 1935 it inspired Sinclair Lewis to title his own anti-authoritarian novel after the commonplace refrain, "It Can't Happen Here."

Of course, as common as this belief may have been, many (including and especially the likes of Orwell and Lewis) knew quite well how misguided it was. Having watched the Nazis transform the German political landscape with little more than well-chosen words and carefully produced propaganda, they understood that the freedom their nations enjoyed was far more fragile than most of their countrymen imagined. This was especially true of Orwell, whose intention while writing *1984* was unapologetically that it should serve as a warning to the democracies of the world about the danger of underestimating the threat of fascism and totalitarian autocracy.

At the core of Orwell's warning in *1984* is the message that propaganda is the absolute root of all tyranny, and a nation can only be free to the extent that it keeps propaganda from flourishing. In the universe of *1984*, nearly every aspect of society is bent around upholding Big Brother's propaganda machine, with large sectors of the government dedicated to falsifying documents, erasing evidence, and managing the intricate paper trails of the regime's latest campaign of deception.

In many ways, this mirrored what was happening in socialist totalitarian states like the USSR and China, and provided a clear message to the democratic societies of the world: The key to warding off autocracy and fascism is preventing government from creating a monopoly on information. As long as you uphold freedom of expression and allow for the existence of a free and independent press, no government can successfully perpetrate the kind of propaganda necessary for totalitarian tyranny to take hold.

Thankfully, during the decades that succeeded the publication of *1984*, the major western democracies of the world have seemed to heed Orwell's advice. While these vital freedoms of speech and expression have certainly come under attack throughout the years, they have not yet succumbed to an assault, and as a result the forces of authoritarianism and oppression have never gained more than a momentary foothold.

Then, as the twentieth century gave way to the twenty-first, the Internet happened.

Of course, the arrival of the Internet transformed every aspect of the way society created, consumed, and disseminated information, taking away control of the media from a small number of broadcasters and publishers and giving it over to anyone with a computer. At first, it seemed as if this great democratization of information could finally deal a fatal blow to the threat of autocracy and fascism forever. After all, with the ability to create and distribute media now available to everyone, how could any government ever hope to control enough of a nation's information to successfully undermine the truth and perpetrate the kind of propaganda necessary for an authoritarian regime to wield power?

Unfortunately, it hasn't quite worked out that way so far.

Instead of becoming a steadfast, decentralized beacon of the truth, it can be argued that the Internet has instead only made the truth become less relevant than ever before. Given such a variety of contradictory information, many people have simply lost faith in the truth, merely through the act of trying to figure out where to find it. And when the truth becomes irrelevant, there no longer exists any need for would-be tyrants to create a monopoly on information at all. On the contrary, they merely need to make their propaganda more attractive than the truth to achieve the same result. In the end, we are left with a reality that not even Orwell could have imagined: given the choice between truth and propaganda, in a free and open market of ideas, many people are choosing to believe the propaganda.

So now, more than any time since Orwell first put pen to paper about that bright cold day in April, we yet again find ourselves keenly aware of the fragility of our freedom, and tasked by history once more to protect it.

Luckily, the means and methods that despots have used throughout history to establish their tyrannies have been carefully documented so that we might know how to recognize and resist them. It is towards this end that the five sections of this book have been organized.

In "Fake News and Alternative Facts," the quotations focus on the how despots utilize propaganda, and the importance of a free press in the fight against tyranny. In "Bad Hombres," the quotations center around the nature of fear and prejudice and how these emotions are manufactured and manipulated to foment division and justify oppression. "Draining the Swamp" focuses on the dysfunctional relationship between politics and corruption that is inherent in every authoritarian regime, while "Order and Strength" collects quotations on the ways that tyrants trample on rights and liberties in their ruthless pursuits of power. The final section of this book is the only one that is not about how to recognize tyranny; it is about how to resist it. In "Resistance," you will find words of wisdom that are both practical and inspirational, and all collected with the purpose of spurring readers to take action against anyone who would dare to resurrect the scourge of fascism and exploit it once again.

Like *1984*, this book makes no apologies about its intentions: its sole ambition is to call on the voices of the past to warn you about the present, in the hopes that you will fight for our future.

James Ryan Daley
Editor

Fake News and Alternative Facts

(Or, Quotations on Propaganda, Lies, and Freedom of the Press)

"Negative polls are fake news."

"Russia is fake news."

"You are fake news."

—Donald J. Trump, 45th President of the United States of America (b. 1946)

"But the most brilliant propagandist technique will yield no success unless one fundamental principle is borne in mind constantly and with unflagging attention. It must confine itself to a few points and repeat them over and over. Here, as so often in this world, persistence is the first and most important requirement for success."

—Adolf Hitler, German Chancellor and leader of the Nazi Party (1889 – 1945)

"Alternative facts are not facts. They are falsehoods."

—Chuck Todd, American broadcast journalist (b. 1972)

☉

"In the end the Party would announce that two and two made five, and you would have to believe it. It was inevitable that they should make that claim sooner or later: the logic of their position demanded it. Not merely the validity of experience, but the very existence of external reality, was tacitly denied by their philosophy. The heresy of heresies was common sense."

—George Orwell, English author and essayist (1903 – 1950), from *1984*

☉

"Those who are capable of tyranny are capable of perjury to sustain it."

—Lysander Spooner, American anarchist and political philosopher (1808 – 1887)

☉

"The result of a consistent and total substitution of lies for factual truth is not that the lie will now be accepted as truth and truth be defamed as a lie, but that the sense by which we take our bearings in the real world—and the category of truth versus falsehood is among the mental means to this end—is being destroyed."

—Hannah Arendt, German-American political theorist (1906 – 1975)

"Against stupidity the very gods themselves contend in vain."
—Friedrich von Schiller, German playwright and philosopher
(1759 – 1805)

◉

"When widely followed public figures feel free to say anything,
without any fact-checking, it becomes impossible for a democracy to think intelligently about big issues."
—Thomas L. Friedman, American journalist and author (b. 1953)

◉

"But better to get hurt by the truth than comforted with a lie."
—Khaled Hosseini, Afghan-born American novelist (b. 1965)

◉

"Where is there dignity unless there is honesty?"
—Cicero, Roman philosopher and rhetorician (106 – 43 BC)

◉

"When one with honeyed words but evil mind persuades the
mob, great woes befall the state."
—Euripides, Greek dramatist (480 – 406 BC)

◉

"The peculiar evil of silencing the expression of an opinion is,
that it is robbing the human race; posterity as well as the existing generation; those who dissent from the opinion, still more
than those who hold it. If the opinion is right, they are deprived
of the opportunity of exchanging error for truth: if wrong, they

lose, what is almost as great a benefit, the clearer perception and livelier impression of truth, produced by its collision with error."

—John Stuart Mill, English philosopher and political economist (1806 – 1873)

"A free press is not a privilege but an organic necessity in a great society."

—Walter Lippmann, American political commentator (1889 – 1974)

"There is nothing in the record of the past two years when both Houses of Congress have been controlled by the Republican Party which can lead any person to believe that those promises will be fulfilled in the future. They follow the Hitler line—no matter how big the lie; repeat it often enough and the masses will regard it as truth."

—John F. Kennedy, 35th President of the United States of America (1917 – 1963)

"Human beings live in their myths. They only endure their realities."

—Robert Anton Wilson, American novelist (1932 – 2007)

"Those who corrupt the public mind are just as evil as those who steal from the public purse."

—Adlai Stevenson II, American politician and diplomat (1900 – 1965)

"There is one freedom on which all other liberties depend and that is freedom of expression, freedom of speech, of print. If this is taken away, no other freedom can exist, or at least it would be soon suppressed."

—Leszek Kołakowski, Polish philosopher (1927 – 2009)

◉

"You don't need people's opinion on a fact. You might as well have a poll asking: 'Which number is bigger, 15 or 5?' or 'Do owls exist?' or 'Are there hats?'"

—John Oliver, English comedian and political commentator (b. 1977)

◉

"Nothing in all the world is more dangerous than sincere ignorance and conscientious stupidity."

—Martin Luther King, Jr., American Baptist minister and civil rights activist (1929 – 1968)

◉

"The obvious types of American fascists are dealt with on the air and in the press. These demagogues and stooges are fronts for others. Dangerous as these people may be, they are not so significant as thousands of other people who have never been mentioned. The American fascist would prefer not to use violence. His method is to poison the channels of public information. With a fascist the problem is never how best to present the truth to the public but how best to use the news to deceive the public into giving the fascist and his group more money or more power."

—Henry A. Wallace, 33rd Vice President of the United States of America (1888 – 1965)

●

"It is part of the price of leadership of this great and free nation to be the target of clever satirists."

—Lyndon B. Johnson, 36th President of the United States of America (1908 – 1973)

●

"Before mass leaders seize the power to fit reality to their lies, their propaganda is marked by its extreme contempt for facts as such, for in their opinion fact depends entirely on the power of man who can fabricate it."

—Hannah Arendt, German-American political theorist (1906 – 1975)

●

"Propaganda is to a democracy what the bludgeon is to a totalitarian state."

—Noam Chomsky, American linguist and political activist (b. 1928)

●

"I'm not going to censor myself to comfort your ignorance."

—Jon Stewart, American comedian and political commentator (b. 1962)

"No persons are more frequently wrong, than those who will not admit they are wrong."

—François de La Rochefoucauld, French author (1613 – 1680)

◉

"A free press can of course be good or bad, but, most certainly, without freedom it will never be anything but bad."

—Albert Camus, French existentialist author and playwright (1913 – 1960)

◉

"I have always been among those who believed that the greatest freedom of speech was the greatest safety, because if a man is a fool, the best thing to do is to encourage him to advertise the fact by speaking."

—Woodrow Wilson, 28th President of the United States of America (1856 – 1924)

◉

"Repetition does not transform a lie into a truth."

—Franklin D. Roosevelt, 32nd President of the United States of America (1882 – 1945)

◉

"Truthiness is tearing apart our country, and I don't mean the argument over who came up with the word. I don't know whether it's a new thing, but it's certainly a current thing, in that it doesn't seem to matter what facts are. It used to be, everyone was entitled to their own opinion, but not their own facts. But that's not the case anymore. Facts matter not at all. Perception is everything."

—Stephen Colbert, American comedian and television host (b. 1964)

"Men are so simple of mind, and so much dominated by their immediate needs, that a deceitful man will always find plenty who are ready to be deceived."

—Niccolò Machiavelli, Italian political philosopher (1469 – 1527)

"The free press is the mother of all our liberties and of our progress under liberty."

—Adlai Stevenson II, American politician and diplomat (1900 – 1965)

"In my view, far from deserving condemnation for their courageous reporting, the *New York Times*, the *Washington Post* and other newspapers should be commended for serving the purpose that the Founding Fathers saw so clearly."

—Justice Hugo L. Black, American politician and Associate Justice of the U. S. Supreme Court (1886 – 1971)

"The greatest friend of Truth is time, her greatest enemy is Prejudice, and her constant companion Humility."

—Charles Caleb Colton, English author and clergyman (1780 – 1832)

"It would not be impossible to prove with sufficient repetition and a psychological understanding of the people concerned that a square is in fact a circle. They are mere words, and words can be molded until they clothe ideas and disguise."

—Joseph Goebbels, Minister of Propaganda during Nazi control of Germany (1897 – 1945)

◉

"Against logic there is no armor like ignorance."

—Laurence J. Peter, Canadian educator and author (1919 – 1990)

◉

"The true hypocrite is the one who ceases to perceive his deception, the one who lies with sincerity."

—André Gide, French author (1869 – 1951)

◉

"Unthinking respect for authority is the greatest enemy of truth."

—Albert Einstein, German-born theoretical physicist (1879 – 1955)

◉

"The right to be heard does not automatically include the right to be taken seriously."

—Hubert H. Humphrey, 38th Vice President of the United States of America (1911 – 1978)

"I think if the people of this country can be reached with the truth, their judgment will be in favor of the many, as against the privileged few."

—Eleanor Roosevelt, First Lady of the United States of America (1884 – 1962)

"Truth is the cry of all, but the game of the few."

—Bishop George Berkeley, Irish philosopher (1685 – 1753)

"Truthfulness has never been counted among the political virtues, and lies have always been regarded as justifiable tools in political dealings."

—Hannah Arendt, German-American political theorist (1906 – 1975)

"But all was false and hollow; though his tongue
Dropped manna, and could make the worse appear
The better reason."

—John Milton, English poet (1608 – 1674)

"He is one of those orators of whom it was well said, 'Before they get up, they do not know what they are going to say; when they are speaking, they do not know what they are saying; and when they sit down they do not know what they have said.'"

—Winston Churchill, English statesman and Prime Minister (1874 – 1965)

"If Satan ever laughs, it must be at hypocrites; they are the greatest dupes he has."

—Charles Caleb Colton, English author and clergyman (1780 – 1832)

●

"When it comes to controlling human beings there is no better instrument than lies. Because, you see, humans live by beliefs. And beliefs can be manipulated. The power to manipulate beliefs is the only thing that counts."

—Michael Ende, German novelist (1929 – 1995), from *The Neverending Story*

●

"A popular Government, without popular information, or the means of acquiring it, is but a Prologue to a Farce or a Tragedy; or perhaps, both. Knowledge will forever govern ignorance: And a people who mean to be their own Governors must arm themselves with the power which knowledge gives."

—James Madison, 4th President of the United States of America (1751 – 1836)

●

"Talking much about oneself may be a way of hiding oneself."

—Friedrich Nietzsche, German philosopher (1844 – 1900)

●

"As scarce as truth is, the supply has always been in excess of the demand."

—Josh Billings, American humorist author (1818 – 1885)

"Debate on public issues should be uninhibited, robust, and wide-open, and that it may well include vehement, caustic, and sometimes unpleasantly sharp attacks on government and public officials."

—Justice William J. Brennan, Jr., American lawyer and Associate Justice of the U. S. Supreme Court (1906 – 1997), *New York Times Co. v. Sullivan*, 1964

"Nothing really succeeds which is not based on reality; sham, in a large sense, is never successful. In the life of the individual, as in the more comprehensive life of the State, pretension is nothing and power is everything."

—Edwin Percy Whipple, American essayist (1819 – 1886)

"We are apt to shut our eyes against a painful truth, and listen to the song of that siren till she transforms us into beasts."

—Patrick Henry, American politician orator (1736 – 1799)

"Everything that deceives may be said to enchant."

—Plato, Greek philosopher (c. 427 – 347 BC)

"We become slaves the moment we hand the keys to the definition of reality entirely over to someone else, whether it is a business, an economic theory, a political party, the White House, Newsworld or CNN."

—B. W. Powe, Canadian poet and author (b. 1955)

"One great error is that we suppose mankind more honest than they are."

—Alexander Hamilton, American statesman (1755 – 1804)

"You may fool all the people some of the time; you can even fool some of the people all the time; but you can't fool all of the people all the time."

—Abraham Lincoln, 16th President of the United States of America (1809 – 1865), attributed

"Now, what I want is Facts. Teach these boys and girls nothing but Facts. Facts alone are wanted in life. Plant nothing else, and root out everything else. You can only form the minds of reasoning animals upon Facts: nothing else will ever be of any service to them. This is the principle on which I bring up my own children, and this is the principle on which I bring up these children. Stick to Facts, sir!"

—Charles Dickens, English author (1812 – 1870), from *Hard Times*

"You don't have to fool all the people all of the time; you just have to fool enough to get elected."

—Gerald Barzan, American humorist and author

"It's discouraging to think how many people are shocked by honesty and how few by deceit."

—Noël Coward, English Playwright (1899 – 1973)

●

"If decade after decade the truth cannot be told, each person's mind begins to roam irretrievably. One's fellow countrymen become harder to understand than Martians."

—Alexander Solzhenitsyn, Russian author and historian (1918 – 2008)

●

"He who does not bellow the truth when he knows the truth makes himself the accomplice of liars and forgers."

—Charles Pierre Péguy, French poet and essayist (1873 – 1914)

●

"Truth is treason in the empire of lies."

—Ron Paul, American politician (b. 1935)

●

"One of the saddest lessons of history is this: If we've been bamboozled long enough, we tend to reject any evidence of the bamboozle. We're no longer interested in finding out the truth. The bamboozle has captured us. It's simply too painful to acknowledge, even to ourselves, that we've been taken. Once you give a charlatan power over you, you almost never get it back."

—Carl Sagan, American astronomer and author (1934 – 1996)

"He who knows how to flatter also knows how to slander."
—Napoléon Bonaparte, French military leader and Emperor of the French (1769 – 1821)

●

"The truth may be stretched thin, but it never breaks, and it always surfaces above lies, as oil floats on water."
—Miguel de Cervantes, Spanish novelist (1547 – 1616), from *Don Quixote*

●

"You can't adopt politics as a profession and remain honest."
—Louis McHenry Howe, American journalist and advisor to President Franklin D. Roosevelt (1871 – 1936)

●

"False words are not only evil in themselves, but they infect the soul with evil."
—Socrates, Greek philosopher (c. 469 – 399 BC)

●

"The ability to discriminate between that which is true and that which is false is one of the last attainments of the human mind."
—James Fenimore Cooper, American novelist (1789 – 1851)

●

"Were it left to me to decide whether we should have a government without newspapers, or newspapers without a government, I should not hesitate a moment to prefer the latter. But I should mean that every man should receive those papers and be capable of reading them."

—Thomas Jefferson, 3rd President of the United States of America (1743 – 1826)

☉

"And if all others accepted the lie which the Party imposed—if all records told the same tale—then the lie passed into history and became truth. 'Who controls the past,' ran the Party slogan, 'controls the future: who controls the present controls the past.'"

—George Orwell, English author and essayist (1903 – 1950), from *1984*

☉

"It is error alone which needs the support of government. Truth can stand by itself."

—Thomas Jefferson, 3rd President of the United States of America (1743 – 1826)

☉

"Rather than love, than money, than fame, give me truth."

—Henry David Thoreau, American essayist, poet, and philosopher (1817 – 1862)

☉

"Freedom of the press is guaranteed only to those who own one."

—A. J. Liebling, American journalist (1904 – 1963)

☉

"I tell you, in my opinion, the cornerstone of democracy is free press—that's the cornerstone. I'm convinced if the press . . . it was not possible, of course, but if the free press existed through this century, there wouldn't be Hitler, there wouldn't Stalin, there wouldn't be all this incredible price people have to pay for their freedom, you know, because that's what they're always first after . . . newspapers, radio, television, everything like that."

—Miloš Forman, Czech film director (b. 1932)

👁

"Truth, Sir, is a cow which will yield such people no more milk, and so they are gone to milk the bull."

—Samuel Johnson, English author and critic (1709 – 1784)

👁

"I visit Fox News every now and again, and it's nice, because the Eye of Mordor is above the building."

—Jon Stewart, American comedian and political commentator (b. 1962)

👁

"Let us begin by committing ourselves to the truth, to see it like it is and to tell it like it is, to find the truth, to speak the truth and live with the truth. That's what we'll do."

—Richard Milhous Nixon, 37th President of the United States of America (1913 – 1994)

👁

"God offers to every mind its choice between truth and repose. Take which you please—you can never have both."

—Ralph Waldo Emerson, American transcendentalist essayist and poet (1803 – 1882)

"You see, I always divide people into two groups. Those who live by what they know to be a lie, and those who live by what they believe, falsely, to be the truth."

—Christopher Hampton, English playwright, screenwriter, and director (b. 1946)

☉

"Freedom is the freedom to say that two plus two make four. If that is granted, all else follows."

—George Orwell, English author and essayist (1903 – 1950), from *1984*

☉

"The freedom of the press is one of the greatest bulwarks of liberty, and can never be restrained but by despotic governments."

—George Mason, American politician (1725 – 1792)

☉

"The truth which makes men free is for the most part the truth which men prefer not to hear."

—Herbert Agar, American journalist and historian (1897 – 1980)

☉

"But I suppose the most revolutionary act one can engage in is . . . to tell the truth."

—Howard Zinn, American historian and social activist (1922 – 2010)

"Every communist has a fascist frown, every fascist a communist smile."

—Muriel Spark, Scottish poet and novelist (1918 – 2006)

●

"There is one sacred rule of journalism. The writer must not invent. The legend on the license must read: None Of This Was Made Up."

—John Richard Hersey, American journalist (1914 – 1993)

●

"Facts were never pleasing to him. He acquired them with reluctance and got rid of them with relief. He was never on terms with them until he had stood them on their heads."

—Sir J. M. Barrie, Scottish author; creator of Peter Pan (1860 – 1937)

●

"Political language . . . is designed to make lies sound truthful and murder respectable, and to give an appearance of solidity to pure wind."

—George Orwell, English author and essayist (1903 – 1950)

●

"One may smile, and smile, and be a villain."

—William Shakespeare, English playwright (1564 – 1616), from *Hamlet: Act 1, Scene 5*

"Manipulations of opinion, insofar as they are inspired by well-defined interests, have limited goals; their effect, however, if they happen to touch upon an issue of authentic concern, is no longer subject to their control and may easily produce consequences they never foresaw or intended."

—Hannah Arendt, German-American political theorist (1906 – 1975)

◉

"Facts do not cease to exist because they are ignored."

—Aldous Huxley, English author and essayist (1894 – 1963)

◉

"No one ever went broke underestimating the intelligence of the American people."

—H. L. Mencken, American satirist and cultural critic (1880 – 1956)

◉

"You can fool too many of the people too much of the time."

—James Thurber, American cartoonist and author (1894 – 1961)

◉

"Man's mind is so formed that it is far more susceptible to false-hood than to truth."

—Erasmus, Dutch theologian and Catholic priest (1466 – 1536)

◉

"If you want truth to go round the world you must hire an express train to pull it; but if you want a lie to go round the world, it will fly: it is as light as a feather, and a breath will carry it. It is well said in the old proverb, 'a lie will go round the world while truth is pulling its boots on.'"

—Charles Haddon Spurgeon, English Baptist preacher (1834 – 1892)

☉

"One of the reasons people hate politics is that truth is rarely a politician's objective. Election and power are."

—Cal Thomas, American columnist and political commentator (b. 1942)

☉

"And if, to be sure, sometimes you need to conceal a fact with words, do it in such a way that it does not become known, or, if it does become known, that you have a ready and quick defence."

—Niccolò Machiavelli, Italian political philosopher (1469 – 1527)

☉

"The whole art of government consists in being honest."

—Thomas Jefferson, 3rd President of the United States of America (1743 – 1826)

☉

"How is the world ruled and how do wars start? Diplomats tell lies to journalists and then believe what they read."

—Karl Kraus, Austrian journalist and critic (1874 – 1936)

☉

"The Senator was vulgar, almost illiterate, a public liar easily detected, and in his 'ideas' almost idiotic, while his celebrated piety was that of a traveling salesman for church furniture, and his yet more celebrated humor the sly cynicism of a country store. Certainly there was nothing exhilarating in the actual words of his speeches, nor anything convincing in his philosophy. His political platforms were only wings of a windmill."

—Sinclair Lewis, American author and playwright (1885 – 1951), from *It Can't Happen Here*

◉

"In the First Amendment, the Founding Fathers gave the free press the protection it must have to fulfill its essential role in our democracy. The press was to serve the governed, not the governors. The Government's power to censor the press was abolished so that the press would remain forever free to censure the Government. The press was protected so that it could bare the secrets of government and inform the people . . . Only a free and unrestrained press can effectively expose deception in government."

—Justice Hugo L. Black, American politician and Associate Justice of the U. S. Supreme Court (1886 – 1971), *New York Times Co. v. United States*

◉

"I don't know if a country where the people are so ignorant of reality and of history, if you can call that a free world."

—Jane Fonda, American actress and activist (b. 1937)

"The threat to men of great dignity, privilege and pretense is not from the radicals they revile; it is from accepting their own myth. Exposure to reality remains the nemesis of the great—a little understood thing."

—John Kenneth Galbraith, Canadian diplomat (1908 – 2006)

●

"There is no well-defined boundary line between honesty and dishonesty."

—O. Henry, American short story writer (1862 – 1910)

●

"Sometimes people hold a core belief that is very strong. When they are presented with evidence that works against that belief, the new evidence cannot be accepted. It would create a feeling that is extremely uncomfortable, called cognitive dissonance. And because it is so important to protect the core belief, they will rationalize, ignore and even deny anything that doesn't fit in with the core belief."

—Frantz Fanon, Martinique-born psychiatrist, activist, and author (1925 – 1961)

●

"The most casual student of history knows that, as a matter of fact, truth does not necessarily vanquish. . . . The cause of truth must be championed, and it must be championed dynamically."

—William F. Buckley, Jr., American conservative author and commentator (1925 – 2008)

"It appeared that there had even been demonstrations to thank Big Brother for raising the chocolate ration to twenty grammes a week. And only yesterday, he reflected, it had been announced that the ration was to be REDUCED to twenty grammes a week. Was it possible that they could swallow that, after only twenty-four hours? Yes, they swallowed it."

—George Orwell, English author and essayist (1903 – 1950), from *1984*

"The invention of printing added a new element of power to the race. From that hour, in a most especial sense, the brain and not the arm, the thinker and not the soldier, books and not kings, were to rule the world; and weapons, forged in the mind, keen-edged and brighter than the sunbeam, were to supplant the sword and the battle-axe."

—Edwin Percy Whipple, American essayist (1819 – 1886)

"The ideal subject of totalitarian rule is not the convinced Nazi or the dedicated communist, but people for whom the distinction between fact and fiction, true and false, no longer exists."

—Hannah Arendt, German-American political theorist (1906 – 1975)

"In the big lie there is always a certain force of credibility; because the broad masses of a nation are always more easily corrupted in the deeper strata of their emotional nature than consciously or voluntarily; and thus in the primitive simplicity of their minds they more readily fall victims to the big lie than the small lie, since they themselves often tell small lies in little matters but would be ashamed to resort to large-scale falsehoods."

—Adolf Hitler, German Chancellor and leader of the Nazi Party (1889 – 1945)

⊙

"Our great democracies still tend to think that a stupid man is more likely to be honest than a clever man, and our politicians take advantage of this prejudice by pretending to be even more stupid than nature made them."

—Bertrand Russell, British philosopher and author (1872 – 1970)

⊙

"The propagandist's purpose is to make one set of people forget that certain other sets of people are human."

—Aldous Huxley, English author and essayist (1894 – 1963)

⊙

"Truth crushed to earth shall rise again."

—William Cullen Bryant, American poet and editor of the *New York Evening Post* (1794 – 1878)

⊙

"It is impossible that a man who is false to his friends and neighbours should be true to the public."

—Bishop George Berkeley, Irish philosopher (1685 – 1753)

"The conscious and intelligent manipulation of the organized habits and opinions of the masses is an important element in democratic society. Those who manipulate this unseen mechanism of society constitute an invisible government which is the true ruling power of our country."

—Edward Bernays, Austrian-born American propagandist, known as the "father of public relations" (1891 – 1995)

❍

"There is a great danger that [the Internet] becomes a place where untruths start to spread more than truths."

—Tim Berners-Lee, English computer scientist; inventor of the World Wide Web (b. 1955)

❍

"The Bush administration is 'impervious to information.'"

—Joe Biden, 47th Vice President of the United States of America (b. 1942)

❍

"In our country the lie has become not just a moral category but a pillar of the State."

—Alexander Solzhenitsyn, Russian author and historian (1918 – 2008)

❍

"Whenever the people are well-informed, they can be trusted with their own government."

—Thomas Jefferson, 3rd President of the United States of America (1743 – 1826)

"Propaganda is a soft weapon: hold it in your hands too long, and it will move about like a snake, and strike the other way."

—Jean Anouilh, French playwright (1910 – 1987)

◉

"Sin has many tools, but a lie is the handle which fits them all."

—Oliver Wendell Holmes, Sr., American poet and polymath (1809 – 1894)

◉

"It is vain to find fault with those arts of deceiving, wherein men find pleasure to be deceived."

—John Locke, English philosopher (1632 – 1704)

◉

"Comment is free, but facts are sacred."

—C. P. Scott, British politician and journalist (1846 – 1932)

◉

"Ignorance is an evil weed, which dictators may cultivate among their dupes, but which no democracy can afford among its citizens."

—William Henry Beveridge, English economist and social reformer (1879 – 1963)

◉

"Facts are stubborn things; and whatever may be our wishes, our inclinations, or the dictates of our passions, they cannot alter the state of facts and evidence."

—John Adams, 2nd President of the United States of America (1735 – 1826)

"What a man had rather were true he more readily believes."
—Francis Bacon, English philosopher, author, and statesman
(1561 – 1626)

●

"If there's one thing I've learned from dealing with politicians over the years, it's that the only thing guaranteed to force them into action is the press—or, more specifically, fear of the press."
—Donald J. Trump, 45th President of the United States of America (b. 1946), from *The Art of the Deal*

Bad Hombres

(Or, Quotations on the Nature of Fear and Prejudice)

"We have some bad hombres here, and we're going to get them out."
—Donald J. Trump, 45th President of the United States of America (b. 1946)

"If he were allowed contact with foreigners he would discover that they are creatures similar to himself and that most of what he has been told about them is lies. The sealed world in which he lives would be broken, and the fear, hatred, and self-righteousness on which his morale depends might evaporate. It is therefore realized on all sides that however often Persia,

or Egypt, or Java, or Ceylon may change hands, the main fron-
tiers must never be crossed by anything except bombs."

—George Orwell, English author and essayist (1903 – 1950),
from *1984*

"I had always hoped that this land might become a safe and
agreeable asylum to the virtuous and persecuted part of mankind, to whatever nation they might belong."

—George Washington, 1st President of the United States of
America (1732 – 1799)

"The whole aim of practical politics is to keep the populace
alarmed (and hence clamorous to be led to safety) by menacing
it with an endless series of hobgoblins, all of them imaginary."

—H. L. Mencken, American satirist and cultural critic (1880 – 1956)

"Ignorance and prejudice are the handmaidens of propaganda.
Our mission, therefore, is to confront ignorance with knowledge, bigotry with tolerance, and isolation with the outstretched
hand of generosity. Racism can, will, and must be defeated."

—Kofi Annan, Ghanaian diplomat and former Secretary-General
of the United Nations (b. 1938)

"Racism is not merely a simplistic hatred. It is, more often, broad sympathy toward some and broader skepticism toward others."

—Ta-Nehisi Coates, American author and educator (b. 1975)

◉

"When and if fascism comes to America it will not be labeled 'made in Germany'; it will not be marked with a swastika; it will not even be called fascism; it will be called, of course, 'Americanism.' . . . For never, probably, has there been a time when there was a more vigorous effort to surround social and international questions with such a fog of distortion and prejudices and hysterical appeal to fear."

—Halford E. Luccock, American scholar and theologian (1885 – 1960)

◉

"Western civilization, Christianity, decency are struggling for their very lives. In this worldwide civil war, race prejudice is our most dangerous enemy, for it is a disease at the very root of our democratic life."

—Mordecai Wyatt Johnson, American pastor and educator (1891 – 1976)

◉

"Prejudice is the child of ignorance."

—William Hazlitt, English author and essayist (1778 – 1830)

"Who does vote for these dishonest shitheads? Who among us can be happy and proud of having all this innocent blood on our hands? Who are these swine? These flag-sucking half-wits who get fleeced and fooled by stupid little rich kids like George Bush? They are the same ones who wanted to have Muhammad Ali locked up for refusing to kill gooks. They speak for all that is cruel and stupid and vicious in the American character. They are the racists and hate mongers among us—they are the Ku Klux Klan. I piss down the throats of these Nazis. And I am too old to worry about whether they like it or not. Fuck them."

—Hunter S. Thompson, American journalist and author (1937 – 2005)

"Before we can study the central issues of life today, we must destroy the prejudices and fallacies born of previous centuries."
—Leo Tolstoy, Russian novelist (1828 – 1910)

"Great spirits have always found violent opposition from mediocrities. The latter cannot understand it when a man does not thoughtlessly submit to hereditary prejudices but honestly and courageously uses his intelligence."
—Albert Einstein, German-born theoretical physicist (1879 – 1955)

"When we begin to build walls of prejudice, hatred, pride, and self-indulgence around ourselves, we are more surely imprisoned

than any prisoner behind concrete walls and iron bars."
—Mother Angelica, American Catholic nun and television host
(1923 – 2016)

"Prejudice is a raft onto which the shipwrecked mind clambers
and paddles to safety."
—Ben Hecht, American author and screenwriter (1894 – 1964)

"Opinions founded on prejudice are always sustained with the
greatest violence."
—Hebrew Proverb

"Every miserable fool who has nothing at all of which he can be
proud, adopts as a last resource pride in the nation to which he
belongs; he is ready and happy to defend all its faults and follies
tooth and nail, thus reimbursing himself for his own inferiority."
—Arthur Schopenhauer, German philosopher (1788 – 1860)

"It's an universal law—intolerance is the first sign of an inad-
equate education. An ill-educated person behaves with arrogant
impatience, whereas truly profound education breeds humility."
—Alexander Solzhenitsyn, Russian author and historian (1918 – 2008)

"There is nothing more frightful than ignorance in action."
—Johann Wolfgang von Goethe, German writer and statesman
(1749 – 1832)

"The very ink with which all history is written is merely fluid prejudice."

—Mark Twain, American author and humorist (1835 – 1910)

"Ignorance gives a sort of eternity to prejudice, and perpetuity to error."

—Reverend Robert Hall, English Baptist minister (1764 – 1831)

"What a sad era when it is easier to smash an atom than a prejudice."

—Albert Einstein, German-born theoretical physicist (1879 – 1955)

"We cannot trample upon the humanity of others without devaluing our own. The Igbo, always practical, put it concretely in their proverb *Onye ji onye n'ani ji onwe ya*: 'He who will hold another down in the mud must stay in the mud to keep him down.'"

—Chinua Achebe, Nigerian novelist and poet (1930 – 2013)

"Our nation is waging a war on a radical network of terrorists—not on a religion, and not a civilization. As we wage this war to defend our principles, we must live up to those principles ourselves. And one of the deepest commitments of America is tolerance. No one should be treated unkindly because of the color of their skin or the content of their creed. No one should be unfairly judged by appearance or ethnic background, or religious faith."

—George W. Bush, 43rd President of the United States of America (b. 1946)

👁

"Prejudice squints when it looks, and lies when it talks."

—Laure Junot, Duchess of Abrantès, French memoirist (1784 – 1838)

👁

"Reason transformed into prejudice is the worst form of prejudice, because reason is the only instrument for liberation from prejudice."

—Allan Bloom, American philosopher (1930 – 1992)

👁

"The most certain test by which we judge whether a country is really free is the amount of security for the minorities."

—Lord Acton, English historian and author (1834 – 1902)

👁

"You can only protect your liberties in this world by protecting the other man's freedom. You can only be free if I am free."

—Clarence Darrow, American lawyer and civil rights advocate (1857 – 1938)

👁

"Prejudice is opinion without judgement."

—Voltaire, French Enlightenment author and philosopher (1694 – 1778)

"I wish I could say that racism and prejudice were only distant memories. We must dissent from the indifference. We must dissent from the apathy. We must dissent from the fear, the hatred and the mistrust . . . We must dissent because America can do better, because America has no choice but to do better."

—Thurgood Marshall, American lawyer and Associate Justice of the U. S. Supreme Court (1908 – 1993)

"It is not our differences that divide us. It is our inability to recognize, accept, and celebrate those differences."

—Audre Lorde, American writer and civil rights activist (1934 – 1992)

"When a man gives his opinion, he's a man. When a woman gives her opinion, she's a bitch."

—Bette Davis, American actress (1908 – 1989)

"Recognize yourself in he and she who are not like you and me."

—Carlos Fuentes, Mexican novelist (1928 – 2012)

"When the judgement's weak, The prejudice is strong."

—Kane O'Hara, Irish composer and playwright (1712 – 1782)

"Love, friendship, respect, do not unite people as much as a common hatred for something."

—Anton Chekhov, Russian author and playwright (1860 – 1904)

"I take issue with many people's description of people being 'Illegal' Immigrants. There aren't any illegal Human Beings as far as I'm concerned."

—Dennis Kucinich, American politician (b. 1946)

◉

"Nationalism is an infantile thing. It is the measles of mankind."

—Albert Einstein, German-born theoretical physicist (1879 – 1955)

◉

"He flattered himself on being a man without any prejudices; and this pretension itself is a very great prejudice."

—Anatole France, French poet and novelist (1844 – 1924)

◉

"The history of men's opposition to women's emancipation is more interesting perhaps than the story of that emancipation itself."

—Virginia Woolf, Modernist English author (1882 – 1941)

◉

"Governments exist to protect the rights of minorities. The loved and the rich need no protection: they have many friends and few enemies."

—Wendell Phillips, American attorney and activist (1811 – 1884)

◉

"Illegal aliens have always been a problem in the United States. Ask any Indian."

—Robert Orben, American speechwriter and humorist (b. 1927)

"When we lose the right to be different, we lose the privilege to be free."

—Charles Evans Hughes, Sr., American author and politician (1862 – 1948)

◉

"Of all the evils for which man has made himself responsible, none is so degrading, so shocking or so brutal as his abuse of the better half of humanity; the female sex."

—Mahatma Gandhi, Indian social activist and leader of the Indian independence movement (1869 – 1948)

◉

"The divide of race has been America's constant curse. Each new wave of immigrants gives new targets to old prejudices. Prejudice and contempt, cloaked in the pretense of religious or political conviction, are no different. They have nearly destroyed us in the past. They plague us still. They fuel the fanaticism of terror. They torment the lives of millions in fractured nations around the world. These obsessions cripple both those who are hated and, of course, those who hate, robbing both of what they might become."

—William Jefferson Clinton, 42nd President of the United States of America (b. 1946)

◉

"Prejudice is the reason of fools."

—Voltaire, French Enlightenment author and philosopher (1694 – 1778)

"Denying racism is the new racism."

—Bill Maher, American comedian and political commentator (b. 1956)

◉

"But it makes an immigrant laugh to hear the fears of the nationalist, scared of infection, penetration, miscegenation, when this is small fry, peanuts, compared to what the immigrant fears—dissolution, disappearance."

—Zadie Smith, English author and essayist (b. 1975)

◉

"Everyone's quick to blame the alien."

—Aeschylus, Greek dramatist (525 – 456 BC)

◉

"No prejudice has even been able to prove its case in the court of reason."

—Mark Twain, American author and humorist (1835 – 1910)

◉

"Anyone who calls you 'little lady' has already excluded you from the set of people worth listening to."

—Neil Gaiman, English author (b. 1960)

◉

"The world has never yet seen a truly great and virtuous nation because in the degradation of woman the very fountains of life are poisoned at their source."

—Lucretia Mott, American reformer and women's rights activist (1793 – 1880)

"Many people think they are thinking when they are merely rearranging their prejudices."
—William James, American philosopher and psychologist (1842 – 1910)

"The interaction of disparate cultures, the vehemence of the ideals that led the immigrants here, the opportunity offered by a new life, all gave America a flavor and a character that make it as unmistakable and as remarkable to people today as it was to Alexis de Tocqueville in the early part of the nineteenth century."
—John F. Kennedy, 35th President of the United States of America (1917 – 1963)

"Anger and intolerance are the enemies of correct understanding."
—Mahatma Gandhi, Indian social activist and leader of the Indian independence movement (1869 – 1948)

"The truth is, immigrants tend to be more American than people born here."
—Chuck Palahniuk, American novelist (b. 1962), from *Choke*

"The intensity of the frenzy is the most hopeful feature of this disgraceful exhibition—of hysterical, unintelligent fear—which is quite foreign to the generous American nature. It will pass like the Know-nothing days, but the sense of shame and sin should endure."

—Louis D. Brandeis, American lawyer and Associate Justice of the U. S. Supreme Court (1856 – 1941)

👁

"Justice delayed is justice denied."

—William E. Gladstone, English politician and Prime Minister (1809 – 1898)

👁

"Before I built a wall I'd ask to know
What I was walling in or walling out."

—Robert Frost, American poet (1874 – 1963)

👁

"That is just the way with some people. They get down on a thing when they don't know nothing about it."

—Mark Twain, American author and humorist (1835 – 1910), from *The Adventures of Huckleberry Finn*

👁

"I have fought against white domination, and I have fought against black domination. I have cherished the ideal of a democratic and free society in which all persons will live together in harmony and with equal opportunities. It is an ideal which I hope to live for and achieve. But, if needs be, it is an ideal for which I am prepared to die."

—Nelson Mandela, South African anti-apartheid activist; President of South Africa (1918 – 2013)

"Remember, when the judgment is weak the prejudice is strong."

—Kane O'Hara, Irish composer and playwright (1712 – 1782)

"All animals are equal but some animals are more equal than others."

—George Orwell, English author and essayist (1903 – 1950), from *Animal Farm*

"We still think of a powerful man as a born leader and a powerful woman as an anomaly."

—Margaret Atwood, Canadian poet and novelist (b. 1939)

"Nothing in life is to be feared, it is only to be understood. Now is the time to understand more, so that we may fear less."

—Marie Curie, Polish-born French physicist and chemist (1867 – 1934)

"As you grow older, you'll see white men cheat black men every day of your life, but let me tell you something and don't you forget it—whenever a white man does that to a black man, no matter who he is, how rich he is, or how fine a family he comes from, that white man is trash."

—Harper Lee, American author (1926 – 2016), from *To Kill a Mockingbird*

"How a minority,
Reaching a majority,
Seizing authority,
Hates a minority!"
—Leonard H. Robbins, American poet (1877 – 1947)

◉

"They shouldn't teach their immigrants' kids all about democracy unless they mean to let them have a little bit of it, it only makes for trouble. Me and the United States is dissociating our alliance as of right now, until the United States can find time to read its own textbooks a little."
—James Jones, American novelist (1921 – 1977), from *From Here to Eternity*

◉

"The real problem is that the way that power is given out in our society pits us against each other."
—Anita Hill, American attorney and academic (b. 1956)

◉

"You have to admit that most women who have done something with their lives have been disliked by almost everyone."
—Françoise Gilot, French artist and author (b. 1921)

◉

"Shall we judge a country by the majority, or by the minority? By the minority, surely."
—Ralph Waldo Emerson, American transcendentalist essayist and poet (1803 – 1882)

"A man must be excessively stupid, as well as uncharitable, who believes there is no virtue but on his own side."

—Joseph Addison, English poet, publisher, and politician (1672 – 1719)

◉

"However sugarcoated and ambiguous, every form of authoritarianism must start with a belief in some group's greater right to power, whether that right is justified by sex, race, class, religion or all four. However far it may expand, the progression inevitably rests on unequal power and airtight roles within the family."

—Gloria Steinem, American journalist and political activist (b. 1934)

◉

"We are not descended from fearful men."

—Edward R. Murrow, American broadcast journalist (1908 – 1965)

◉

"For more than forty years I have selected my collaborators on the basis of their intelligence and their character and not on the basis of their grandmothers, and I am not willing for the rest of my life to change this method which I have found so good."

—Fritz Haber, German chemist (1868 – 1934)

◉

"It is part of human nature to hate those whom you have injured."

—Tacitus, Roman senator and historian (54 – 117 AD)

"Fear of something is at the root of hate for others, and hate within will eventually destroy the hater."

—George Washington Carver, Botanist, inventor, and one of the nation's most influential African-American scientists (c. 1864 – 1943)

"Patriotism is a lively sense of collective responsibility. Nationalism is a silly cock crowing on its own dunghill."

—Richard Aldington, English poet and novelist (1892 – 1962), from *The Colonel's Daughter*

"Patriotism is when love of your own people comes first; nationalism, when hate for people other than your own comes first."

—Charles de Gaulle, French general and statesman (1890 – 1970)

"To live anywhere in the world today and be against equality because of race or color is like living in Alaska and being against snow."

—William Faulkner, American novelist (1897 – 1962)

"They [the Irish] are looked upon with contempt for their want of aptitude in learning new things; they're ready and ingenious lying; their eye-service. These are the faults of an oppressed race, which must require the aid of better circumstances through two or three generations to eradicate."

—Margaret Fuller, American journalist and women's rights activist (1810 – 1850)

"We can scarcely hate anyone that we know."

—William Hazlitt, English author and essayist (1778 – 1830)

"Real equality is immensely difficult to achieve, it needs continual revision and monitoring of distributions. And it does not provide buffers between members, so they are continually colliding or frustrating each other."

—Mary Douglas, English anthropologist (1921 – 2007)

"Hatred is the vice of narrow souls; they feed it with all their littlenesses, and make it the pretext of base tyrannies."

—Honoré De Balzac, French novelist and playwright (1799 – 1850)

"If you hate your enemies, you will contract such a vicious habit of mind, as by degrees will break out upon those who are your friends, or those who are indifferent to you."

—Plutarch, Greek biographer (c. 46 – 120 AD)

"The majority has the might—more's the pity—but it hasn't the right. . . . The minority is always right."

—Henrik Ibsen, Norwegian playwright and poet (1828 – 1906)

"Prejudice, a dirty word, and faith, a clean one, have something in common: they both begin where reason ends."

—Harper Lee, American author (1926 – 2016), from *Go Set a Watchman*

"We should therefore claim, in the name of tolerance, the right not to tolerate the intolerant."

—Karl R. Popper, Austrian-born English philosopher (1902 – 1994)

●

"The history of an oppressed people is hidden in the lies and the agreed-upon myths of its conquerors."

—Meridel Le Sueur, American author and poet (1900 – 1996)

●

"A nation is judged by how it treats its minorities."

—Rene Levesque, Canadian journalist and politician (1922 – 1987)

●

"He [Mao Zedong] was, it seemed to me, really a restless fight promoter by nature and good at it. He understood ugly human instincts such as envy and resentment, and knew how to mobilize them for his ends. He ruled by getting people to hate each other."

—Jung Chang, Chinese-born English author (b. 1952)

●

"As those who believe in the visibility of ghosts can easily see them, so it is always easy to see repulsive qualities in those we despise and hate."

—Frederick Douglass, American statesman, author, and abolitionist (1818 – 1895)

"Let me assert my firm belief that the only thing we have to fear is fear itself—nameless, unreasoning, unjustified terror which paralyzes needed efforts to convert retreat into advance."

—Franklin D. Roosevelt, 32nd President of the United States of America (1882 – 1945)

●

"The prejudices of ignorance are more easily removed than the prejudices of interest; the first are all blindly adopted, the second willfully preferred."

—George Bancroft, American statesman and diplomat (1800 – 1891)

●

"The American Negro has the great advantage of having never believed that collection of myths to which white Americans cling: that their ancestors were all freedom-loving heroes, that they were born in the greatest country the world has ever seen, or that Americans are invincible in battle and wise in peace, that Americans have always dealt honorably with Mexicans and Indians and all other neighbors or inferiors, that American men are the world's most direct and virile, that American women are pure."

—James Baldwin, American novelist and essayist (1924 – 1987)

"You can sway a thousand men by appealing to their prejudices quicker than you can convince one man by logic."
—Robert A. Heinlein, American science fiction author (1907 – 1988)

"Populism is on the increase—a populism that rejects anything different, anyone with a different-coloured skin, or a different race or religion. This is the real danger and unspoken risk that threatens to pollute democracy."
—Jacques Delors, French economist and politician (b. 1925)

"Let us not look back in anger, nor forward in fear, but around in awareness."
—James Thurber, American cartoonist and author (1894 – 1961)

"Borders are scratched across the hearts of men
By strangers with a calm, judicial pen,
And when the borders bleed we watch with dread
The lines of ink along the map turn red."
—Marya Mannes, American journalist and critic (1904 – 1990)

"People are pretty much alike. It's only that our differences are more susceptible to definition than our similarities."
—Linda Ellerbee, American journalist (b. 1944)

"Politics, as a practice, whatever its professions, has always been the systematic organization of hatreds."

—Henry Adams, American historian (1838 – 1918)

●

"If a small thing has the power to make you angry, does that not indicate something about your size?"

—Sydney J. Harris, American journalist (1917 – 1986)

●

"In all my work what I try to say is that as human beings we are more alike than we are unalike."

—Maya Angelou, American novelist and poet (1928 – 2014)

●

"You do not wipe away the scars of centuries by saying, 'Now, you are free to go where you want, do what you desire, and choose the leaders you please.' You do not take a man who, for years, has been hobbled by chains, liberate him, bring him to the starting line of the race, saying, 'You are free to compete with the others.'"

—Lyndon B. Johnson, 36th President of the United States of America (1908 – 1973)

●

"Prejudices, it is well known, are most difficult to eradicate from the heart whose soil has never been loosened or fertilized by education; they grow there, firm as weeds among stones."

—Charlotte Brontë, English poet and novelist (1816 – 1855), from *Jane Eyre*

"Every true man has pride of race, and under appropriate circumstances when the rights of others, his equals before the law, are not to be affected, it is his privilege to express such pride and to take such action based upon it as to him seems proper. But I deny that any legislative body or judicial tribunal may have regard to the race of citizens when the civil rights of those citizens are involved."

—Justice John Marshall Harlan, American lawyer and Associate Justice of the U. S. Supreme Court (1833 – 1911)

⊙

"A nation is a society united by a delusion about its ancestry and by common hatred of its neighbours."

—William Ralph Inge, English author and Anglican priest (1860 – 1954)

⊙

"Real freedom is freedom from fear, and unless you can live free from fear you cannot live a dignified human life."

—Aung San Suu Kyi, Burmese politician and diplomat (b. 1945)

⊙

"Human diversity makes tolerance more than a virtue; it makes it a requirement for survival."

—René Dubos, French-born American microbiologist (1901 – 1982)

"The price of hating other human beings is loving oneself less."

—Eldridge Cleaver, American author and political activist (1935 – 1998)

"In America everybody is of the opinion that he has no social superiors, since all men are equal, but he does not admit that he has no social inferiors, for, from the time of Jefferson onward, the doctrine that all men are equal applies only upwards, not downwards."

—Bertrand Russell, British philosopher and author (1872 – 1970)

"Bigotry may be roughly defined as the anger of men who have no opinions."

—G. K. Chesterton, English author and philosopher (1874 – 1936)

"The sure guarantee of the peace and security of each race is the clear, distinct, unconditional recognition by our governments, national and state, of every right that inheres in civil freedom, and of the equality before the law of all citizens of the United States, without regard to race."

—Justice John Marshall Harlan, American lawyer and Associate Justice of the U. S. Supreme Court (1833 – 1911)

"When we leave people out or write them off, we not only shortchange them and their dreams, we shortchange our country and our own futures."

—Hillary Clinton, American politician and First Lady (b. 1947)

"Fear is the main source of superstition, and one of the main sources of cruelty. To conquer fear is the beginning of wisdom."

—Bertrand Russell, British philosopher and author (1872 – 1970)

"There is no room in this country for hyphenated Americanism . . . The one absolutely certain way of bringing this nation to ruin, of preventing all possibility of its continuing to be a nation at all, would be to permit it to become a tangle of squabbling nationalities."

—Theodore Roosevelt, 26th President of the United States of America (1858 – 1919)

"It is not healthy when a nation lives within a nation, as colored Americans are living inside America. A nation cannot live confident of its tomorrow if its refugees are among its citizens."

—Pearl S. Buck, American novelist (1892 – 1973)

"A country is a piece of land surrounded on all sides by boundaries, usually unnatural."

—Joseph Heller, American satirical novelist (1923 – 1999), from *Catch-22*

"Prejudice and self-sufficiency naturally proceed from inexperience of the world and ignorance of mankind."

—Joseph Addison, English poet, publisher, and politician (1672 – 1719)

"There are more things, Lucilius, that frighten us than injure us, and we suffer more in imagination than in reality."

—Seneca the Younger, Roman Stoic philosopher (4 BC – 65 AD)

"His foreparents came to America in immigrant ships. My foreparents came to America in slave ships. But whatever the original ships, we are both in the same boat tonight."

—Jesse Jackson, American civil rights activist (b. 1941)

"For as long as the power of America's diversity is diminished by acts of discrimination and violence against people just because they are black, Hispanic, Asian, Jewish, Muslim or gay, we still must overcome."

—Ron Kind, American politician (b. 1963)

"Fear is the tax that conscience pays to guilt."

—George Sewell, English Actor (1924 – 2007)

"We hate some persons because we do not know them; and we will not know them because we hate them."

—Charles Caleb Colton, English author and clergyman (1780 – 1832)

"We who are liberal and progressive know that the poor are our equals in every sense except that of being equal to us."

—Lionel Trilling, American literary critic (1905 – 1975)

◉

"For happily, the Government of the United States, which gives to bigotry no sanction, to persecution no assistance, requires only that they who live under its protection should demean themselves as good citizens in giving it at all occasions their effectual support."

—George Washington, 1st President of the United States of America (1732 – 1799)

◉

"Hatred is a feeling which leads to the extinction of values."

—José Ortega y Gasset, Spanish philosopher and essayist (1883 – 1955)

◉

"Bigotry dwarfs the soul by shutting out the truth."

—Edwin Hubbell Chapin, American preacher and magazine editor (1814 – 1880)

◉

"Let them hate, so long as they fear."

—Lucius Accius, Roman poet and scholar (170 – 86 BC), attributed

"Do you know what we call opinion in the absence of evidence? We call it prejudice."

—Michael Crichton, American novelist (1942 – 2008), from *State of Fear*

"No democracy can long survive which does not accept as fundamental to its very existence the recognition of the rights of minorities."

—Franklin D. Roosevelt, 32nd President of the United States of America (1882 – 1945)

"I would like to see a time when man loves his fellow man and forgets his colour or his creed. We will never be civilized until that time comes. I know the Negro race has a long road to go. I believe that the life of the Negro race has been a life of tragedy, of injustice, of oppression. The law has made him equal, but man has not."

—Clarence Darrow, American lawyer and civil rights advocate (1857 – 1938)

"No passion so effectually robs the mind of all its powers of acting and reasoning as fear."

—Edmund Burke, Irish statesman (1729 – 1797)

"The overwhelming condemnation makes it clear we have made enormous progress in teaching everyone that racism is bad.

Where we seem to have dropped the ball is in teaching people what racism actually is . . . which allows people to say incredibly racist things while insisting they would never."

—Jon Stewart, American comedian and political commentator (b. 1962)

"Give me your tired, your poor,

Your huddled masses yearning to breathe free,

The wretched refuse of your teeming shore,

Send these, the homeless, tempest-tossed to me,

I lift my lamp beside the golden door!"

—Emma Lazarus, American Poet (1849 – 1887), inscription on the Statue of Liberty

Draining the Swamp

(Or, Quotations on Politics and Corruption)

"So like a month ago I said 'drain the swamp' and the place went crazy. And I said 'Whoa, what's this?' Then I said it again. And then I start saying it like I meant it, right? And then I started to love it, and the place loved it. Drain the swamp. It's true. It's true. Drain the swamp."

—Donald J. Trump, 45th President of the United States of America (b. 1946)

"It doesn't look like they're draining the swamp. . . . If nothing changes, they'll be pouring the swamp into the Oval Office."

—Sheldon Whitehouse, U. S. Senator from Rhode Island (b. 1955)

"A people that elect corrupt politicians, impostors, thieves and traitors are not victims . . . but accomplices."—George Orwell, English author and essayist (1903 – 1950), attributed

●

"He knows nothing; and he thinks he knows everything. That points clearly to a political career."

—George Bernard Shaw, Irish playwright and essayist (1856 – 1950)

●

"You have all the characteristics of a popular politician: a horrible voice, bad breeding, and a vulgar manner."

—Aristophanes, Greek playwright (445 – 385 BC)

●

"In whose delusional mind is democracy made 'better' by allowing wealthy people to control more of it?"

—Jon Stewart, American comedian and political commentator (b. 1962)

●

"The liberty of a democracy is not safe if the people tolerate the growth of private power to a point where it becomes stronger than the democratic state itself. That, in its essence, is Fascism: ownership of Government by an individual, by a group, or any other controlling private power."

—Franklin D. Roosevelt, 32nd President of the United States of America (1882 – 1945)

"The United States Congress, like a lot of rich people, lives in two houses."

—John Green, American novelist (b. 1977)

●

"Absolute power does not corrupt absolutely, absolute power attracts the corruptible."

—Frank Herbert, American author (1920 – 1986)

●

"He has been called a mediocre man; but this is unwarranted flattery. He was a politician of monumental littleness."

—Richard Milhous Nixon, 37th President of the United States of America (1913 – 1994)

●

"It could probably be shown by facts and figures that there is no distinctly native American criminal class except Congress."

—Mark Twain, American author and humorist (1835 – 1910)

●

"Every time we turn our heads the other way when we see the law flouted, when we tolerate what we know to be wrong, when we close our eyes and ears to the corrupt because we are too busy or too frightened, when we fail to speak up and speak out, we strike a blow against freedom and decency and justice."

—Robert F. Kennedy, American politician (1925 – 1968)

"What makes it so plausible to assume that hypocrisy is the vice of vices is that integrity can indeed exist under the cover of all other vices except this one. Only crime and the criminal, it is true, confront us with the perplexity of radical evil; but only the hypocrite is really rotten to the core."

—Hannah Arendt, German-American political theorist (1906 – 1975)

"What power has law where only money rules?"

—Gaius Petronius Arbiter, Roman courtier and author (27 – 66 AD)

"If you look at great human civilizations, from the Roman Empire to the Soviet Union, you will see that most do not fail simply due to external threats but because of internal weakness, corruption, or a failure to manifest the values and ideals they espouse."

—Cory Booker, American politician (b. 1969)

"It's ridiculous to talk about freedom in a society dominated by huge corporations. What kind of freedom is there inside a corporation? They're totalitarian institutions—you take orders from above and maybe give them to people below you. There's about as much freedom as under Stalinism."

—Noam Chomsky, American linguist and political activist (b. 1928)

"As usual, in every scheme that worsens the position of the poor, it is the poor who are invoked as beneficiaries."

—Vandana Shiva, Indian scholar and activist (b. 1952)

◉

"When they call the roll in the Senate, the Senators do not know whether to answer 'Present' or 'Not Guilty.'"

—Theodore Roosevelt, 26th President of the United States of America (1858 – 1919)

◉

"The worst disease in the world today is corruption. And there is a cure: transparency."

—Bono, Irish singer-songwriter (b. 1960)

◉

"All you need in this life is ignorance and confidence; then success is sure."

—Mark Twain, American author and humorist (1835 – 1910)

◉

"If we define an American fascist as one who in case of conflict puts money and power ahead of human beings, then there are undoubtedly several million fascists in the United States."

—Henry A. Wallace, 33rd Vice President of the United States of America (1888 – 1965)

◉

"Hypocrisy is the audacity to preach integrity from a den of corruption."

—Wes Fesler, American athlete and coach (1908 – 1989)

"There is no more dangerous menace to civilization than a government of incompetent, corrupt, or vile men."
—Ludwig von Mises, Austrian economist (1881 – 1973)

☉

"Power does not corrupt men; fools, however, if they get into a position of power, corrupt power."
—George Bernard Shaw, Irish playwright and essayist (1856 – 1950)

☉

"Corrupt politicians make the other ten percent look bad."
—Henry Kissinger, American diplomat (b. 1923)

☉

"When plunder becomes a way of life for a group of men in a society, over the course of time they create for themselves a legal system that authorizes it and a moral code that glorifies it."
—Frédéric Bastiat, French economist (1801 – 1850)

☉

"A man who has never gone to school may steal a freight car; but if he has a university education, he may steal the whole railroad."
—Theodore Roosevelt, 26th President of the United States of America (1858 – 1919)

☉

"Choose a leader who will invest in building bridges, not walls. Books, not weapons. Morality, not corruption. Intellectualism and wisdom, not ignorance. Stability, not fear and terror. Peace, not chaos. Love, not hate. Convergence, not segregation. Tolerance, not discrimination. Fairness, not hypocrisy. Substance, not superficiality. Character, not immaturity. Transparency, not secrecy. Justice, not lawlessness. Environmental improvement and preservation, not destruction. Truth, not lies."

—Suzy Kassem, American writer and poet (b. 1975)

☉

"Power does not corrupt. Fear corrupts . . . perhaps the fear of a loss of power."

—John Steinbeck, American novelist (1902 – 1968)

☉

"All kings is mostly rapscallions."

—Mark Twain, American author and humorist (1835 – 1910), from *The Adventures of Huckleberry Finn*

☉

"Hypocrisy is the most difficult and nerve-racking vice that any man can pursue; it needs an unceasing vigilance and a rare detachment of spirit. It cannot, like adultery or gluttony, be practised at spare moments; it is a whole-time job."

—W. Somerset Maugham, English novelist and playwright (1874 – 1965)

☉

"Wherever you see a man who gives someone else's corruption, someone else's prejudice as a reason for not taking action himself, you see a cog in The Machine that governs us."

—John Jay Chapman, American Author (1862 – 1933)

"Men are more often bribed by their loyalties and ambitions than money."

—Robert H. Jackson, American lawyer and Associate Justice of the U. S. Supreme Court (1892 – 1954)

◉

"Political history is far too criminal and pathological to be a fit subject of study for the young. Children should acquire their heroes and villains from fiction."

—W. H. Auden, English poet (1907 – 1973)

◉

"The accomplice to the crime of corruption is frequently our own indifference."

—Bess Myerson, American politician, television actress, and columnist (1924 – 2014)

◉

"A passion for politics stems usually from an insatiable need, either for power, or for friendship and adulation, or a combination of both."

—Fawn M. Brodie, American biographer (1915 – 1981)

◉

"A reformer is a guy who rides through a sewer in a glass-bottomed boat."

—Jimmy Walker, American politician; Mayor of New York during prohibition (1881 – 1946)

"Giving money and power to government is like giving whiskey and car keys to teenage boys."

—P. J. O'Rourke, American political journalist (b. 1947)

◉

"Laws are like spider's webs: if some poor weak creature come up against them, it is caught; but a bigger one can break through and get away."

—Solon, Athenian statesman and poet (c. 638 – 558 BC)

◉

"It only takes a politician believing in what he says for others to stop believing him."

—Jean Baudrillard, French Semiologist (1929 – 2007)

◉

"Laws grind the poor, and rich men rule the law."

—Oliver Goldsmith, Irish novelist and playwright (1728 – 1774)

◉

"The value systems of those with access to power and of those far removed from such access cannot be the same. The viewpoint of the privileged is unlike that of the underprivileged."

—Aung San Suu Kyi, Burmese politician and diplomat (b. 1945)

◉

"No government, any more than an individual, will long be respected without being truly respectable."

—James Madison, 4th President of the United States of America (1751 – 1836)

"One of the penalties for refusing to participate in politics is that you end up being governed by your inferiors."

—Plato, Greek philosopher (c. 427 – 347 BC)

"Of all the sources of human pride, mere wealth is the basest and most vulgar-minded. Real gentlemen are almost invariably above this low feeling."

—James Fenimore Cooper, American novelist (1789 – 1851)

"The modern conservative is engaged in one of man's oldest exercises in moral philosophy; that is, the search for a superior moral justification for selfishness."

—John Kenneth Galbraith, Canadian diplomat (1908 – 2006)

"When one may pay out over two million dollars to presidential and Congressional campaigns, the U. S. government is virtually up for sale."

—John W. Gardner, U. S. Secretary of Health, Education, and Welfare under President Lyndon Johnson (1912 – 2002)

"Those who foolishly sought power by riding the back of the tiger ended up inside."

—John F. Kennedy, 35th President of the United States of America (1917 – 1963)

"I have come to the conclusion that politics are too serious a matter to be left to the politicians."

—Charles de Gaulle, French general and statesman (1890 – 1970)

⊙

"When a man tells you that he got rich through hard work, ask him: 'Whose?'"

—Don Marquis, American humorist and author (1878 – 1937)

⊙

"Evil when we are in its power is not felt as evil but as a necessity, or even a duty."

—Simone Weil, French philosopher and activist (1909 – 1943)

⊙

"The surface of American society is covered with a layer of democratic paint, but from time to time one can see the old aristocratic colors breaking through."

—Alexis de Tocqueville, French diplomat (1805 – 1859)

⊙

"I sit on a man's back, choking him and making him carry me, and yet assure myself and others that I am very sorry for him and wish to ease his lot by all possible means—except by getting off his back."

—Leo Tolstoy, Russian novelist (1828 – 1910)

⊙

"The desire of power in excess caused the angels to fall."

—Francis Bacon, English philosopher, author, and statesman (1561 – 1626)

"Those who have been once intoxicated with power, and have derived any kind of emolument from it, even though but for one year, never can willingly abandon it."

—Edmund Burke, Irish statesman (1729 – 1797)

"Guard against the impostures of pretended patriotism."

—George Washington, 1st President of the United States of America (1732 – 1799)

"Do you not know, my son, with how little wisdom the world is governed?"

—Axel Oxenstierna, Swedish Statesman (1583 – 1654)

"What I worry about would be that you essentially have two chambers, the House and the Senate, but you have simply, majoritarian, absolute power on either side. And that's just not what the founders intended."

—Barack Obama, 44th President of the United States of America (b. 1961)

"The first method for estimating the intelligence of a ruler is to look at the men he has around him."

—Niccolò Machiavelli, Italian political philosopher (1469 – 1527)

"Corruption, the most infallible symptom of constitutional liberty."

—Edward Gibbon, English historian and politician (1737 – 1794)

●

"It's difficult to get a man to understand something when his salary depends upon his not understanding it."

—Upton Sinclair, American novelist (1878 – 1968)

●

"Things fall apart; the center cannot hold;

Mere anarchy is loosed upon the world,

The blood-dimmed tide is loosed, and everywhere

The ceremony of innocence is drowned;

The best lack all conviction, while the worst

Are full of passionate intensity."

—W. B. Yeats, Irish poet (1865 – 1939)

●

"Power tends to corrupt, and absolute power corrupts absolutely. Great men are almost always bad men . . . There is no worse heresy than that the office sanctifies the holder of it."

—Lord Acton, English historian and author (1834 – 1902)

●

"Power without a nation's confidence is nothing."

—Catherine the Great, Empress of Russia (1729 – 1796)

"Any institution which does not suppose the people good, and the magistrate corruptible is evil."

—Maximilien Robespierre, French politician and leader during the French Revolution (1758 – 1794)

"A nation never falls but by suicide."

—Ralph Waldo Emerson, American transcendentalist essayist and poet (1803 – 1882)

"We are living in a world where greed has become for the wealthiest people their own religion, and they make no apologies for it."

—Bernie Sanders, American politician (b. 1941)

"Inconsistencies of opinion arising from changes of circumstance are often justifiable. But there is one sort of inconsistency that is culpable: it is the inconsistency between a man's conviction and his vote, between his conscience and his conduct."

—Daniel Webster, American politician and statesman (1782 – 1852)

"So long as men worship the Caesars and Napoleons, Caesars and Napoleons will duly arise and make them miserable."

—Aldous Huxley, English author and essayist (1894 – 1963)

"Remember, democracy never lasts long. It soon wastes, exhausts, and murders itself. There never was a democracy yet that did not commit suicide."

—John Adams, 2nd President of the United States of America (1735 – 1826)

●

"When the president does it, that means that it is not illegal."

—Richard Milhous Nixon, 37th President of the United States of America (1913 – 1994)

●

"Politics is perhaps the only profession for which no preparation is thought necessary."

—Robert Louis Stevenson, Scottish novelist and travel writer (1850 – 1894)

●

"A party is perpetually corrupted by personality."

—Ralph Waldo Emerson, American transcendentalist essayist and poet (1803 – 1882)

●

"Power is the most persuasive rhetoric."

—Friedrich von Schiller, German playwright and philosopher (1759 – 1805)

"If we desire respect for the law, we must first make the law respectable."

—Louis D. Brandeis, American lawyer and Associate Justice of the U. S. Supreme Court (1856 – 1941)

☉

"Ironically, women who acquire power are more likely to be criticized for it than are the men who have always had it."

—Carolyn Heilbrun, American academic and activist (1926 – 2003)

☉

"We have a cancer within, close to the presidency, that is growing. It is growing daily."

—John W. Dean III, White House Counsel for Richard Nixon; plead guilty to obstruction of justice during the Watergate scandal (b. 1938)

☉

"Money is the mother's milk of politics."

—Jesse Unruh, American politician (1922 – 1987)

☉

"I have a fantasy where Ted Turner is elected President but refuses because he doesn't want to give up power."

—Arthur C. Clarke, British author (1917 – 2008)

☉

"The man who goes into politics because he needs the money isn't likely to do as much harm as the man who goes into it

merely because he has money to burn."
—Philander C. Johnson, American journalist and humorist (1866 – 1939)

☉

"An honest politician is one who when he's bought stays bought."
—Simon Cameron, American politician (1799 – 1889)

☉

"The production of wealth is not the work of any one man, and the acquisition of great fortunes is not possible without the cooperation of multitudes of men; . . . therefore the individuals to whose lot these fortunes fall . . . should never lose sight of the fact that as they hold them by the will of society expressed in statute law, so they should administer them as trustees for the benefit of society as inculcated by moral law."
—Peter Cooper, American industrialist (1791 – 1883)

☉

"Being powerful is like being a lady. If you have to tell people you are, you aren't."
—Margaret Thatcher, English politician and Prime Minister (1925 – 2013)

☉

"Power is action; the electoral principle is discussion. No political action is possible when discussion is permanently established."
—Honoré De Balzac, French novelist and playwright (1799 – 1850)

"Whenever a man has cast a longing eye on offices, a rottenness begins in his conduct."

—Thomas Jefferson, 3rd President of the United States of America (1743 – 1826)

"No man undertakes a trade he has not learned, even the meanest; yet everyone thinks himself sufficiently qualified for the hardest of all trades—that of government."

—Socrates, Greek philosopher (c. 469 – 399 BC)

"Politics is the art of turning influence into affluence."

—Philander C. Johnson, American journalist and humorist (1866 – 1939)

"Not even a collapsing world looks dark to a man who is about to make his fortune."

—E. B. White, American author and editor (1899 – 1985)

"Among a people generally corrupt, liberty cannot long exist."

—Edmund Burke, Irish statesman (1729 – 1797)

"The ordinary fair-weather patriot goes out upon the street corners, and in public places, and proclaims his love for American institutions as a cloak for the support for existing wrongs, which

make him rich and great; he uses his patriotism as he does the other tools with which he plies his trade; patriotism to him does not mean devotion to his country and the people's highest good, but a blind, unthinking worship of things as they are; the constitution and laws, to him, are to be either enforced or broken as it may profit at the time; his is a patriotism that flies an American flag from the schoolhouse, and sacrifices the most vital and fundamental principles of liberty for gain."
—Clarence Darrow, American lawyer and civil rights advocate (1857 – 1938)

"Politics is not the art of the possible. It consists in choosing between the disastrous and the unpalatable."
—John Kenneth Galbraith, Canadian diplomat (1908 – 2006)

"Power is always dangerous. Power attracts the worst and corrupts the best."
—Edward Abbey, American author and environmental activist (1927 – 1989)

"The louder he talked of his honour, the faster we counted our spoons."
—Ralph Waldo Emerson, American transcendentalist essayist and poet (1803 – 1882)

"Vote: the instrument and symbol of a freeman's power to make a fool of himself and a wreck of his country."

—Ambrose Bierce, American author and journalist (1842 – 1914)

●

"We'd all like to vote for the best man, but he's never a candidate."

—Kin Hubbard, American cartoonist (1868 – 1930)

●

"When I was a boy I was told that anybody could become President; I'm beginning to believe it."

—Clarence Darrow, American lawyer and civil rights advocate (1857 – 1938)

Order and Strength

(Or, Quotations on Fascism, Oppression, and Tyranny)

"I like order. I like things done in an orderly manner. And certainly the Germans, that's something that they're rather well known for. But I do, I like order and I like strength."
—Donald J. Trump, 45th President of the United States of America (b. 1946), in response to an interviewer asking if there was anything typically German about his character

"Now I will tell you the answer to my question. It is this. The Party seeks power entirely for its own sake. We are not interested in the good of others; we are interested solely in power, pure power. What pure power means you will understand presently. We are different from the oligarchies of the past in that we know what we are doing. All the others, even those who resembled ourselves, were cowards and hypocrites. The

German Nazis and the Russian Communists came very close to us in their methods, but they never had the courage to recognize their own motives. They pretended, perhaps they even believed, that they had seized power unwillingly and for a limited time, and that just around the corner there lay a paradise where human beings would be free and equal. We are not like that. We know that no one ever seizes power with the intention of relinquishing it. Power is not a means; it is an end. One does not establish a dictatorship in order to safeguard a revolution; one makes the revolution in order to establish the dictatorship. The object of persecution is persecution. The object of torture is torture. The object of power is power. Now you begin to understand me."

—George Orwell, English author and essayist (1903 – 1950), from *1984*

◉

"We cannot expect people to have respect for law and order until we teach respect to those we have entrusted to enforce those laws."

—Hunter S. Thompson, American journalist and author (1937 – 2005)

◉

"Fascism is not in itself a new order of society. It is the future refusing to be born."

—Aneurin Bevan, Welsh politician (1897 – 1916)

"Still another danger is represented by those who, paying lip service to democracy and the common welfare, in their insatiable greed for money and the power which money gives, do not hesitate surreptitiously to evade the laws designed to safeguard the public from monopolistic extortion. Their final objective toward which all their deceit is directed is to capture political power so that, using the power of the state and the power of the market simultaneously, they may keep the common man in eternal subjection. They claim to be super-patriots, but they would destroy every liberty guaranteed by the Constitution. They are patriotic in time of war because it is to their interest to be so, but in time of peace they follow power and the dollar wherever they may lead."

—Henry A. Wallace, 33rd Vice President of the United States of America (1888 – 1965)

◉

"What difference does it make to the dead, the orphans and the homeless, whether the mad destruction is wrought under the name of totalitarianism or in the holy name of liberty or democracy?"

—Mahatma Gandhi, Indian social activist and leader of the Indian independence movement (1869 – 1948)

"The greatest dangers to liberty lurk in the insidious encroachment by men of zeal—well-meaning but without understanding."
—Louis D. Brandeis, American lawyer and Associate Justice of the U. S. Supreme Court (1856 – 1941)

☉

"I believe in benevolent dictatorship provided I am the dictator."
—Richard Branson, English entrepreneur and philanthropist (b. 1950)

☉

"Fascism appeals alike to those elements among the younger minded middle class who are conservative by temperament and strongly nationalist in spirit, and to those rarer and more dynamic elements who, naturally revolutionary in their outlook, have been disappointed and exasperated by the failure of all leadership from the left to approach any fulfilment of their aspiration."
—W. E. D. Allen, English politician and chief propagandist for the British Union of Fascists (1901 – 1973)

☉

"Power in America today is control of the means of communication."
—Theodore White, American political journalist (1915 – 1986)

☉

"How, then, did it rise? My explanation is simple—but it will require you to think carefully. I'll argue that fascism is a product of extremism—of both the left and right. That extremism broke the center—which created a vacuum in which rose New Fascists, who combine the worst elements of both left and right."

—Umair Haque, Economist (b. 1981)

"It was during those long and lonely years that my hunger for the freedom of my own people became a hunger for the freedom of all people, white and black. I knew as well as I knew anything that the oppressor must be liberated just as surely as the oppressed. A man who takes away another man's freedom is a prisoner of hatred, he is locked behind the bars of prejudice and narrow-mindedness. I am not truly free if I am taking away someone else's freedom, just as surely as I am not free when my freedom is taken from me. The oppressed and the oppressor alike are robbed of their humanity."

—Nelson Mandela, South African anti-apartheid activist; President of South Africa (1918 – 2013)

"The true danger is when liberty is nibbled away, for expedience, and by parts."

—Edmund Burke, Irish statesman (1729 – 1797)

"In Germany, the Nazis came for the Communists and I didn't speak up because I was not a Communist. Then they came for the Jews and I didn't speak up because I was not a Jew. Then they came for the trade unionists and I didn't speak up because I was not a trade unionist. Then they came for the Catholics and I was a Protestant so I didn't speak up. Then they came for me . . . By that time there was no one to speak up for anyone."

—Martin Niemöller, German pastor and anti-Nazi activist (1892 – 1984)

"The same state of the passions which fits the multitude, who have not sufficient stock of reason and knowledge to guide them, for opposition to tyranny and oppression, very naturally leads them to a contempt and disregard of all authority."

—Alexander Hamilton, American statesman (1755 – 1804)

"There is a quality even meaner than outright ugliness or disorder, and this meaner quality is the dishonest mask of pretended order, achieved by ignoring or suppressing the real order that is struggling to exist and to be served."

—Jane Jacobs, American author and activist (1916 – 2006)

"What Orwell failed to predict was that we'd buy the cameras ourselves, and that our biggest fear would be that nobody was watching."

—Keith Lowell Jensen, American comedian (b. 1972)

"Nothing appears more surprising to those who consider human affairs with a philosophical eye, than the easiness with which the many are governed by the few."

—David Hume, Scottish philosopher (1711 – 1776)

◉

"Eternal vigilance is the price of liberty—power is ever stealing from the many to the few."

—Wendell Phillips, American attorney and activist (1811 – 1884)

◉

"There will come a time when it isn't 'They're spying on me through my phone' anymore. Eventually, it will be 'My phone is spying on me.'"

—Philip K. Dick, American science fiction author (1928 – 1982)

◉

"If you don't have a seat at the table, you're probably on the menu."

—Elizabeth Warren, American politician (b. 1949)

◉

"To announce that there must be no criticism of the President, or that we are to stand by the President, right or wrong, is not only unpatriotic and servile, but is morally treasonable to the American public."

—Theodore Roosevelt, 26th President of the United States of America (1858 – 1919)

"Social conservatism and neoconservatism have revived authoritarian conservatism, and not for the better of conservatism or American democracy. True conservatism is cautious and prudent. Authoritarianism is rash and radical. American democracy has benefited from true conservatism, but authoritarianism offers potentially serious trouble for any democracy."

—John W. Dean III, White House Counsel for Richard Nixon; plead guilty to obstruction of justice during the Watergate scandal (b. 1938)

"You see what power is—holding someone else's fear in your hand and showing it to them!"

—Amy Tan, American author (b. 1952)

"Fascism is not just a word. It's not just a way to insult someone with whom you disagree. It is a specific thing. It is a specific form of far right politics that involves a sort of narcissistic cult of superman action around the leader of the party."

—Rachel Maddow, American political broadcast journalist (b. 1973)

"Justice without force is powerless; force without justice is tyrannical."

—Blaise Pascal, French scientist and philosopher (1623 – 1662)

"The cost of liberty is less than the price of repression."

—W. E. B. Du Bois, American civil rights activist (1868 – 1963)

◉

"The measure of a man is what he does with power."

—Plato, Greek philosopher (c. 427 – 347 BC)

◉

"The essence of fascism is to make laws forbidding everything and then enforce them selectively against your enemies."

—John Lescroart, American novelist (b. 1948)

◉

"Fascism should more appropriately be called Corporatism because it is a merger of state and corporate power."

—Benito Mussolini, Italian Prime Minister and leader of the National Fascist Party (1883 – 1945)

◉

"What should move us to action is human dignity: the inalienable dignity of the oppressed, but also the dignity of each of us. We lose dignity if we tolerate the intolerable."

—Dominique de Menil, French art collector and philanthropist (1908 – 1997)

◉

"I really am a pessimist. I've always felt that fascism is a more natural governmental condition than democracy. Democracy is a grace. It's something essentially splendid because it's not at all routine or automatic. Fascism goes back to our infancy and childhood, where we were always told how to live. We were told,

Yes, you may do this; no, you may not do that. So the secret of fascism is that it has this appeal to people whose later lives are not satisfactory."

—Norman Mailer, American author and essayist (1923 – 2007)

"They who can give up essential liberty to obtain a little temporary safety deserve neither liberty nor safety."

—Benjamin Franklin, American Statesman (1706 – 1790)

"I am not free while any woman is unfree, even when her shackles are very different from my own."

—Audre Lorde, American writer and civil rights activist (1934 – 1992)

"Ultimately, totalitarianism is the only sort of politics that can truly serve the sky-god's purpose. Any movement of a liberal nature endangers his authority and that of his delegates on earth. One God, one King, one Pope, one master in the factory, one father-leader in the family at home."

—Gore Vidal, American author and intellectual (1925 – 2012)

"Once a government is committed to the principle of silencing the voice of opposition, it has only one way to go, and that is down the path of increasingly repressive measures, until it becomes a source of terror to all its citizens and creates a country where everyone lives in fear."

—Harry S. Truman, 33rd President of the United States of America (1884 – 1972)

◉

"The first truth is that the liberty of a democracy is not safe if the people tolerate the growth of private power to a point where it becomes stronger than their democratic state itself. That, in its essence, is fascism—ownership of government by an individual, by a group, or by any other controlling private power. . . . Among us today a concentration of private power without equal in history is growing."

—Franklin D. Roosevelt, 32nd President of the United States of America (1882 – 1945)

◉

"Confronted with the choice, the American people would choose the policeman's truncheon over the anarchist's bomb."

—Spiro T. Agnew, 39th Vice President of the United States of America (1918 – 1996)

◉

"No, you can't deny women their basic rights and pretend it's about your 'religious freedom.' If you don't like birth control, don't use it. Religious freedom doesn't mean you can force others to live by your own beliefs."

—Barack Obama, 44th President of the United States of America (b. 1961)

"Fascism is capitalism plus murder."

—Upton Sinclair, American novelist (1878 – 1968)

"Whether the mask is labeled fascism, democracy, or dictator-ship of the proletariat, our great adversary remains the appara-tus—the bureaucracy, the police, the military. Not the one facing us across the frontier of the battle lines, which is not so much our enemy as our brothers' enemy, but the one that calls itself our protector and makes us its slaves. No matter what the cir-cumstances, the worst betrayal will always be to subordinate our-selves to this apparatus and to trample underfoot, in its service, all human values in ourselves and in others."

—Simone Weil, French philosopher and activist (1909 – 1943)

"The essence of Government is power; and power, lodged as it must be in human hands, will ever be liable to abuse."

—James Madison, 4th President of the United States of America (1751 – 1836)

"Oppression can only survive through silence."

—Carmen de Monteflores, American author and activist (b. 1933)

"We thought, because we had power, we had wisdom."

—Stephen Vincent Benét, American poet and novelist (1898 – 1943)

"No state, no government exists. What does in fact exist is a man, or a few men, in power over many men."

—Rose Wilder Lane, American novelist and political theorist (1886 – 1968)

◉

"Man and fascism cannot co-exist. If fascism conquers, man will cease to exist and there will remain only man-like creatures that have undergone an internal transformation. But if man, man who is endowed with reason and kindness, should conquer, then Fascism must perish, and those who have submitted to it will once again become people."

—Vasily Grossman, Soviet Russian writer and journalist (1905 – 1964)

◉

"It is not unfrequent to hear men declaim loudly upon liberty, who, if we may judge by the whole tenor of their actions, mean nothing else by it but their own liberty,—to oppress without control or the restraint of laws all who are poorer or weaker than themselves."

—Samuel Adams, American statesman and political philosopher (1722 – 1803)

◉

"Power is dangerous unless you have humility."

—Richard J. Daley, American politician; mayor of Chicago for twenty-one years (1902 – 1976)

"The enemies of Freedom do not argue; they shout and they shoot."

—Dean Inge, English author and Anglican priest (1860 – 1954)

☉

"I shall be an autocrat: that's my trade. And the good Lord will forgive me: that's his."

—Catherine the Great, Empress of Russia (1729 – 1796)

☉

"Dictatorships foster oppression, dictatorships foster servitude, dictatorships foster cruelty; more abominable is the fact that they foster idiocy."

—Jorge Luis Borges, Argentine poet and short-story writer (1899 – 1986)

☉

"It is an observation no less just than common, that there is no stronger test of a man's real character than power and authority, exciting, as they do, every passion, and discovering every latent vice."

—Plutarch, Greek biographer (45 – 120 AD)

☉

"The earth is the mother of all people, and all people should have equal rights upon it. You might as well expect the rivers to run backward as that any man who was born a free man should be contented when penned up and denied liberty."

—Joseph the Younger, Native American Chief of the Wallowa band of the Nez Perce Tribe (1840 – 1904)

"As for being a General, well, at the age of four with paper hats and wooden swords we're all Generals. Only some of us never grow out of it."

—Peter Ustinov, English actor (1921 – 2004)

◉

"We observe that nothing creates fascists like the threat of freedom."

—Roger Ebert, American film critic (1942 – 2013), from his review of *Pleasantville*, 1998

◉

"It is true that liberty is precious—so precious that it must be rationed."

—Vladimir Ilyich Lenin, First leader of the USSR (1870 – 1924)

◉

"Whoever is new to power is always harsh."

—Aeschylus, Greek dramatist (525 – 456 BC)

◉

"[Hitler] must blood his hounds and show them sport, or else, like Actaeon of old, be devoured by them."

—Winston Churchill, English statesman and Prime Minister (1874 – 1965)

◉

"Generally, nobody behaves decently when they have power."

—Kingsley Amis, English novelist (1922 – 1995)

"A Stalin functionary admitted, 'Innocent people were arrested: naturally—otherwise no one would be frightened. If people, he said, were arrested only for specific misdemeanours, all the others would feel safe and so become ripe for treason.'"

—Paul Johnson, English author and journalist (b. 1928)

●

"There is no good or evil, there is only power, and those too weak to seek it."

—J. K. Rowling, English novelist (b. 1965), from *Harry Potter and the Sorcerer's Stone*

●

"Those who want the Government to regulate matters of the mind and spirit are like men who are so afraid of being murdered that they commit suicide to avoid assassination."

—Harry S. Truman, 33rd President of the United States of America (1884 – 1972)

●

"The greater the state, the more wrong and cruel its patriotism, and the greater is the sum of suffering upon which its power is founded."

—Leo Tolstoy, Russian novelist (1828 – 1910)

●

"But the secret of intellectual excellence is the spirit of criticism; it is intellectual independence. And this leads to difficulties which must prove insurmountable for any kind of authoritarianism. The authoritarian will in general select those who obey, who believe, who respond to his influence. But in doing so, he is bound to select mediocrities. For he excludes those who revolt, who doubt, who dare to resist his influence. Never can an authority admit that the intellectually courageous, i. e. those who dare to defy his authority, may be the most valuable type. Of course, the authorities will always remain convinced of their ability to detect initiative. But what they mean by this is only a quick grasp of their intentions, and they will remain for ever incapable of seeing the difference."

—Karl R. Popper, Austrian-born English philosopher (1902 – 1994)

◉

"Society needs laws. While anarchy can often turn a humdrum weekend into something unforgettable, eventually the mob must be kept from stealing the conch and killing Piggy. And while it would be nice if that 'something' was simple human decency, anybody who has witnessed the '50% Off Wedding Dress Sale' at Filene's Basement knows we need a backup plan—preferably in writing. On the other hand, too many laws can result in outright tyranny, particularly if one of those laws is 'Kneel before Zod.' Somewhere between these two extremes lies the legislative sweet-spot that produces just the right amount of laws for a well-adjusted society—more than zero, less than fascism."

—Jon Stewart, American comedian and political commentator (b. 1962)

"A nation does not have to be cruel to be tough."

—Franklin D. Roosevelt, 32nd President of the United States of America (1882 – 1945)

◉

"All ambitions are lawful except those which climb upward on the miseries or credulities of mankind."

—Joseph Conrad, English novelist (1857 – 1924)

◉

"Those who deny freedom to others deserve it not for themselves, and, under a just God, cannot long retain it."

—Abraham Lincoln, 16th President of the United States of America (1809 – 1865)

◉

"I am more and more convinced that man is a dangerous creature; and that power, whether vested in many or a few, is ever grasping, and like the grave, cries 'Give, give!'"

—Abigail Adams, First Lady of the United States of America (1744 – 1818)

◉

"As nightfall does not come at once, neither does oppression. In both instances, there is a twilight when everything remains seemingly unchanged. And it is in such twilight that we all must be most aware of change in the air—however slight—lest we become unwitting victims of the darkness."

—William O. Douglas, American lawyer and Associate Justice of the U. S. Supreme Court (1898 – 1980)

"Never allow a person to tell you no who doesn't have the power to say yes."

—Eleanor Roosevelt, First Lady of the United States of America (1884 – 1962)

◉

"If we don't believe in freedom of expression for people we despise, we don't believe in it at all."

—Noam Chomsky, American linguist and political activist (b. 1928)

◉

"Power will intoxicate the best hearts, as wine the strongest heads. No man is wise enough, nor good enough to be trusted with unlimited power."

—Charles Caleb Colton, English author and clergyman (1780 – 1832)

◉

"Either none of mankind possesses genuine rights, or everyone shares them equally; whoever votes against another's rights, whatever his religion, colour or sex, forswears his own."

—Marie Jean Antoine Nicolas de Caritat, Marquis of Condorcet, French philosopher and scientist (1743 – 1794)

◉

"Power exercised with violence has seldom been of long duration, but temper and moderation generally produce permanence in all things."

—Seneca the Younger, Roman Stoic philosopher (4 BC – 65 AD)

"A free America . . . means just this: individual freedom for all, rich or poor, or else this system of government we call democracy is only an expedient to enslave man to the machine and make him like it."

—Frank Lloyd Wright, American architect (1867 – 1959)

"It is a miserable state of mind to have few things to desire and many things to fear; and yet that commonly is the case of kings."

—Francis Bacon, English philosopher, author, and statesman (1561 – 1626)

"And on the pedestal these words appear:
'My name is Ozymandias, king of kings:
Look on my works, ye Mighty, and despair!'
Nothing beside remains. Round the decay
Of that colossal wreck, boundless and bare
The lone and level sands stretch far away."

—Percy Bysshe Shelley, English Romantic poet (1792 – 1822)

"Every crisis offers you extra desired power."

—William Moulton Marston, American comic book author; creator of Wonder Woman (1893 – 1947)

"The way to have power is to take it."

—Boss Tweed, American politician and Democratic Party leader (1823 – 1878)

"I will have this done, so I order it done; let my will replace reasoned judgement."

—Juvenal, Roman poet (c. 1st century to 2nd century AD)

◉

"It is better that a man should tyrannize over his bank balance than over his fellow citizens."

—John Maynard Keynes, English economist (1883 – 1946)

◉

"Dictators ride to and fro upon tigers which they dare not dismount. And the tigers are getting hungry."

—Winston Churchill, English statesman and Prime Minister (1874 – 1965)

◉

"The fact is, what I hated in the Church was what I hated in society. Namely, authoritarians. Power freaks. Rigid dogmatists. Those greedy, underloved, undersexed twits who want to run everything. While the rest of us are busy living—busy tasting and testing and hugging and kissing and goofing and growing—they are busy taking over."

—Tom Robbins, American novelist (b. 1932), from *Another Roadside Attraction*

◉

"'Freedom from fear' could be said to sum up the whole philosophy of human rights."

—Dag Hammarskjöld, Swedish diplomat and economist (1905 – 1961)

"A leader is best

When people barely know that he exists,

Not so good when people obey and acclaim him,

Worst when they despise him."

—Lao-tzu, Chinese philosopher (604 – 531 BC)

"The word Fascism has now no meaning except in so far as it signifies 'something not desirable' . . . In the case of a word like democracy, not only is there no agreed definition, but the attempt to make one is resisted from all sides. It is almost universally felt that when we call a country democratic we are praising it: consequently the defenders of every kind of regime claim that it is a democracy, and fear that they might have to stop using the word if it were tied down to any one meaning."

—George Orwell, English author and essayist (1903 – 1950)

"There are no 'human' oppressors. Oppressors have lost their humanity."

—Bernie Sanders, American politician (b. 1941)

"Today in Britain, a fascist has won an election. Can you imagine how we feel? I am a proud and loyal man, madam. We had so much faith in this country. In the war, I thought it is time to help Britain to save democracy and fight fascism. They don't

remember what we did, three million of us fought as volunteers remember—in the desert, in Burma. It makes me so sad."
—Rajinder Singh, Maharaja of Patiala (b. 1946)

👁

"When one has been threatened with a great injustice, one accepts a smaller as a favour."
—Jane Welsh Carlyle, (1801 – 1866)

👁

"We have, I fear, confused power with greatness."
—Stewart Udall, American politician (1920 – 2010)

👁

"There is danger from all men. The only maxim of a free government ought to be to trust no man living with power to endanger the public liberty."
—John Adams, 2nd President of the United States of America (1735 – 1826)

👁

"All, too, will bear in mind this sacred principle, that though the will of the majority is in all cases to prevail, that will to be rightful must be reasonable; that the minority possess their equal rights, which equal law must protect, and to violate would be oppression."
—Thomas Jefferson, 3rd President of the United States of America (1743 – 1826)

"An honest man can feel no pleasure in the exercise of power over his fellow citizens."

—Thomas Jefferson, 3rd President of the United States of America (1743 – 1826)

◉

"No man will make a great leader who wants to do it all himself, or to get all the credit for doing it."

—Andrew Carnegie, American industrialist (1835 – 1919)

◉

"Oppression makes the wise man mad."

—Robert Browning, English poet and playwright (1812 – 1889)

◉

"Bad laws are the worst sort of tyranny."

—Edmund Burke, Irish statesman (1729 – 1797)

◉

"From the equality of rights springs identity of our highest interests; you cannot subvert your neighbor's rights without striking a dangerous blow at your own."

—Carl Schurz, German-born U. S. politician and statesman (1829 – 1906)

◉

"Tyranny is always better organized than freedom."

—Charles Pierre Péguy, French poet and essayist (1873 – 1914)

"Power is so apt to be insolent and Liberty to be saucy, that they are seldom upon good Terms."

—Lord Halifax, English politician (1881 – 1959)

◉

"The love of liberty is the love of others; the love of power is the love of ourselves."

—William Hazlitt, English author and essayist (1778 – 1830)

◉

"Authority has always attracted the lowest elements in the human race. All through history mankind has been bullied by scum."

—P. J. O'Rourke, American political journalist (b. 1947)

◉

"If you want a picture of the future, imagine a boot stamping on a human face—for ever."

—George Orwell, English author and essayist (1903 – 1950), from *1984*

◉

"To satisfy their hunger for meaning and value, they [the masses] turn to such doctrines as nationalism, fascism and revolutionary communism. Philosophically and scientifically, these doctrines are absurd; but for the masses in every community, they have this great merit: they attribute the meaning and value that have been taken away from the world as a whole to the particular part of the world in which the believers happen to be living."

—Aldous Huxley, English author and essayist (1894 – 1963)

"I love power. But it is as an artist that I love it. I love it as a musician loves his violin, to draw out its sounds and chords and harmonies."

—Napoleon Bonaparte, French military leader and Emperor of the French (1769 – 1821)

"All rights tend to declare themselves absolute to their logical extreme. Yet all in fact are limited by the neighborhood of principles of policy which are other than those on which the particular right is founded, and which become strong enough to hold their own when a certain point is reached."

—Justice Oliver Wendell Holmes, Jr., American lawyer and Associate Justice of the U. S. Supreme Court (1841 – 1935)

"The most potent weapon in the hands of the oppressor is the mind of the oppressed."

—Steve Biko, South African anti-apartheid activist (1946 – 1977)

"Half of the harm that is done in this world
Is due to people who want to feel important."

—T. S. Eliot, English poet and author (1888 – 1965)

"There are more instances of the abridgement of the freedom of the people by gradual and silent encroachments of those in power than by violent and sudden usurpations."

—James Madison, 4th President of the United States of America (1751 – 1836)

"Tyranny, like hell, is not easily conquered."

—Thomas Paine, American political theorist and revolutionary (1737 – 1809)

Resistance

"Our opponents, the media and the whole world will soon see as we begin to take further actions, that the powers of the president to protect our country are very substantial and will not be questioned."
—Stephen Miller, senior advisor to Donald J. Trump, (b. 1985)

○

"It is the first responsibility of every citizen to question authority."
—Benjamin Franklin, American Statesman (1706 – 1790)

○

"The history of liberty is the history of resistance."
—Woodrow Wilson, 28th President of the United States of America (1856 – 1924)

○

"Protest is when I say I don't like this. Resistance is when I put an end to what I don't like. Protest is when I say I refuse to go along with this anymore. Resistance is when I make sure everybody else stops going along too."

—Ulrike Marie Meinhof, German militant political activist (1934 – 1976)

☉

"In a time of deceit, telling the truth is a revolutionary act."

—George Orwell, English author and essayist (1903 – 1950), attributed

☉

"We must not confuse dissent with disloyalty. When the loyal opposition dies, I think the soul of America dies with it."

—Edward R. Murrow, American broadcast journalist (1908 – 1965)

☉

"To spend one's life being angry, and in the process doing nothing to change it, is to me ridiculous. I could be mad all day long, but if I'm not doing a damn thing, what difference does it make?"

—Charles Fuller, Jr., American playwright (b. 1939)

☉

"It does not take a majority to prevail . . . but rather an irate, tireless minority, keen on setting brushfires of freedom in the minds of men."

—Samuel Adams, American statesman and political philosopher (1722 – 1803)

"Because it's no longer enough to be a decent person. It's no longer enough to shake our heads and make concerned grimaces at the news. True enlightened activism is the only thing that can save humanity from itself."

—Joss Whedon, American screenwriter, director, and author (b. 1964)

"The country is in deep trouble. We've forgotten that a rich life consists fundamentally of serving others, trying to leave the world a little better than you found it. We need the courage to question the powers that be, the courage to be impatient with evil and patient with people, the courage to fight for social justice. In many instances we will be stepping out on nothing, and just hoping to land on something. But that's the struggle. To live is to wrestle with despair, yet never allow despair to have the last word."

—Cornel West, American intellectual, author, and civil rights activist (b. 1953)

"Liberty lies in the hearts of men and women; when it dies there, no constitution, no law . . . no court can save it. . . . The spirit of liberty is the spirit which is not too sure that it is right; the spirit of liberty is the spirit which seeks to understand the minds of other men and women."

—Learned Hand, American jurist and judicial philosopher (1872 – 1961)

"The only way we'll get freedom for ourselves is to identify our-selves with every oppressed people in the world. We are blood brothers to the people of Brazil, Venezuela, Haiti, Cuba—yes, Cuba too."

—Malcolm X, American civil rights activist (1925 – 1965)

"If everyone demanded peace instead of another television set, then there'd be peace."

—John Lennon, English singer-songwriter (1940 – 1980)

"Everybody can be great . . . because anybody can serve. You don't have to have a college degree to serve. You don't have to make your subject and verb agree to serve. You only need a heart full of grace. A soul generated by love."

—Martin Luther King, Jr., American Baptist minister and civil rights activist (1929 – 1968)

"Better to die fighting for freedom then be a prisoner all the days of your life."

—Bob Marley, Jamaican singer-songwriter (1945 – 1981)

"We must always take sides. Neutrality helps the oppressor, never the victim. Silence encourages the tormentor, never the tormented."

—Elie Wiesel, Romanian-born author, activist, and holocaust survivor (1928 – 2016)

"The people cannot be all, and always, well informed. The part which is wrong will be discontented, in proportion to the importance of the facts they misconceive. If they remain quiet under such misconceptions, it is lethargy, the forerunner of death to the public liberty. . . . What country before ever existed a century and half without a rebellion? And what country can preserve its liberties if their rulers are not warned from time to time that their people preserve the spirit of resistance? Let them take arms. The remedy is to set them right as to facts, pardon and pacify them. What signify a few lives lost in a century or two? The tree of liberty must be refreshed from time to time with the blood of patriots and tyrants. It is its natural manure."

—Thomas Jefferson, 3rd President of the United States of America (1743 – 1826)

"The problems we face, did not come down from the heavens. They are made, they are made by bad human decisions, and good human decisions can change them."

—Bernie Sanders, American politician (b. 1941)

"The President is merely the most important among a large number of public servants. He should be supported or opposed exactly to the degree which is warranted by his good conduct or bad conduct, his efficiency or inefficiency in rendering loyal, able, and disinterested service to the Nation as a whole. Therefore it is absolutely necessary that there should be full liberty to tell the truth about his acts, and this means that it is exactly necessary to blame him when he does wrong as to praise him when he does right. Any other attitude in an American citizen is both base and servile. To announce that there must be no criticism of the President, or that we are to stand by the President, right or wrong, is not only unpatriotic and servile, but is morally treasonable to the American public. Nothing but the truth should be spoken about him or anyone else. But it is even more important to tell the truth, pleasant or unpleasant, about him than about anyone else."

—Theodore Roosevelt, 26th President of the United States of America (1858 – 1919)

◉

"It is better to die on your feet than to live on your knees."

—Emiliano Zapata, military leader during the Mexican Revolution (1879 – 1919)

◉

"One has a moral responsibility to disobey unjust laws."

—Martin Luther King, Jr., American Baptist minister and civil rights activist (1929 – 1968)

◉

"Is life so dear, or peace so sweet, as to be purchased at the price of chains and slavery? Forbid it, Almighty God!—I know not what course others may take; but as for me, give me liberty, or give me death!"

—Patrick Henry, American politician orator (1736 – 1799)

"The opposite of love is not hate, it's indifference. The opposite of art is not ugliness, it's indifference. The opposite of faith is not heresy, it's indifference. And the opposite of life is not death, it's indifference."

—Elie Wiesel, Romanian-born author, activist, and holocaust survivor (1928 – 2016)

☉

"Every day I get better at knowing that it is not a choice to be an activist; rather, it is the only way to hold on to the better parts of my human self. It is the only way I can live and laugh without guilt."

—Staceyann Chin, Jamaican-born poet and activist (b. 1972)

☉

"Loyalty to country always. Loyalty to government, when it deserves it."

—Mark Twain, American author and humorist (1835 – 1910)

☉

"Never doubt that a small group of thoughtful, committed, citizens can change the world. Indeed, it is the only thing that ever has."

—Margaret Mead, American cultural anthropologist (1901 – 1978)

☉

"The duty of youth is to challenge corruption."

—Kurt Cobain, American singer-songwriter (1967 – 1994)

"Finally, let us understand that when we stand together, we will always win. When men and women stand together for justice, we win. When black, white and Hispanic people stand together for justice, we win."

—Bernie Sanders, American politician (b. 1941)

◉

"You never change things by fighting the existing reality. To change something, build a new model that makes the existing model obsolete."

—R. Buckminster Fuller, American architect and inventor (1895 – 1983)

◉

"A true revolution of values will soon cause us to question the fairness and justice of many of our past and present policies. . . . A true revolution of values will soon look uneasily on the glaring contrast of poverty and wealth. With righteous indignation, it will look across the seas and see individual capitalists of the West investing huge sums of money in Asia, Africa, and South America, only to take the profits out with no concern for the social betterment of the countries, and say, 'This is not just.' It will look at our alliance with the landed gentry of South America and say, 'This is not just.' The Western arrogance of feeling that it has everything to teach others and nothing to learn from them is not just."

—Martin Luther King, Jr., American Baptist minister and civil rights activist (1929 – 1968)

"To sin by silence, when they should protest, makes cowards of men."

—Ella Wheeler Wilcox, American author and poet (1850 – 1919)

☉

"There are, in every age, new errors to be rectified and new prejudices to be opposed."

—Samuel Johnson, English author and critic (1709 – 1784)

☉

"If you tremble with indignation at every injustice, then you are a comrade of mine."

—Ernesto Che Guevara, Argentine Marxist and leading figure in the Cuban Revolution (1928 – 1967)

☉

"Find out just what people will submit to, and you have found out the exact amount of injustice and wrong which will be imposed upon them; and these will continue until they are resisted with either words or blows, or both. The limits of tyrants are prescribed by the endurance of those whom they oppress."

—Frederick Douglass, American statesman, author, and abolitionist (1818 – 1895)

☉

"There are too many idiots in this world. And having said it, I have the burden of proving it."

—Frantz Fanon, Martinique-born psychiatrist, activist, and author (1925 – 1961)

"What I've learned is that real change is very, very hard. But I've also learned that change is possible—if you fight for it."

—Elizabeth Warren, American politician (b. 1949)

☉

"Protest beyond the law is not a departure from democracy; it is absolutely essential to it."

—Howard Zinn, American historian and social activist (1922 – 2010)

☉

"If I can't dance to it, it's not my revolution."

—Emma Goldman, Anarchist political activist and author (1869 – 1940)

☉

"There may be times when we are powerless to prevent injustice, but there must never be a time when we fail to protest."

—Elie Wiesel, Romanian-born author, activist, and holocaust survivor (1928 – 2016)

☉

"Justice will not be served until those who are unaffected are as outraged as those who are."

—Benjamin Franklin, American Statesman (1706 – 1790)

☉

"I love America more than any other country in the world and, exactly for this reason, I insist on the right to criticize her perpetually."

—James Baldwin, American novelist and essayist (1924 – 1987)

"People should not be afraid of their government. Governments should be afraid of their people."

—Alan Moore, American writer and comic book author (b. 1953), from *V for Vendetta*

◉

"To accept your country without betraying it, you must love it for that which shows what it might become. America—this monument to the genius of ordinary men and women, this place where hope becomes capacity, this long, halting turn of 'no' into the 'yes'—needs citizens who love it enough to re-imagine and re-make it."

—Cornel West, American intellectual, author, and civil rights activist (b. 1953)

◉

"If you are a woman, if you're a person of colour, if you are gay, lesbian, bisexual, transgender, if you are a person of size, if you are a person of intelligence, if you are a person of integrity, then you are considered a minority in this world. And it's going to be really hard to find messages of self-love and support anywhere. Especially women's and gay men's culture. It's all about how you have to look a certain way or else you're worthless. You know when you look in the mirror and you think 'oh, I'm so fat, I'm so old, I'm so ugly,' don't you know, that's not your authentic self? But that is billions upon billions of dollars of advertising, magazines, movies, billboards, all geared to make you feel shitty about yourself so that you will take your hard earned money and spend it at the mall on some turn-around creme that doesn't turn around shit. When you don't have self-esteem you will hesitate before you do anything in your life. You will hesitate to go for the job you really wanna go for, you will hesitate to ask for a raise, you will hesitate to call yourself an American, you will hesitate to report a rape, you will hesitate to defend yourself when you are discriminated against because of your race, your sexuality, your size, your gender. You will hesitate to vote, you will hesitate to dream. For us to have self-esteem is truly an act of revolution and our revolution is long overdue."

—Margaret Cho, American comedian (b. 1968)

"Those who profess to favor freedom and yet depreciate agitation, are people who want crops without ploughing the ground; they want rain without thunder and lightning; they want the ocean without the roar of its many waters. The struggle may be a moral one, or it may be a physical one, or it may be both. But it must be a struggle. Power concedes nothing without a demand. It never did and it never will."

—Frederick Douglass, American statesman, author, and abolitionist (1818 – 1895)

"Nothing strengthens authority so much as silence."

—Leonardo da Vinci, Italian artist, engineer, and scientist (1452 – 1519)

"True revolution comes from true revulsion; when things get bad enough the kitten will kill the lion."

—Charles Bukowski, American poet (1920 – 1994)

"If by a 'Liberal' they mean someone who looks ahead and not behind, someone who welcomes new ideas without rigid reactions, someone who cares about the welfare of the people—their health, their housing, their schools, their jobs, their civil rights and their civil liberties—someone who believes we can break through the stalemate and suspicions that grip us in our policies abroad, if that is what they mean by a 'Liberal,' then I'm proud to say I'm a 'Liberal.'"

—John F. Kennedy, 35th President of the United States of America (1917 – 1963)

"If I were to remain silent, I'd be guilty of complicity."

—Albert Einstein, German-born theoretical physicist (1879 – 1955)

"The Destiny of Man is to unite, not to divide. If you keep on dividing you end up as a collection of monkeys throwing nuts at each other out of separate trees."

—T. H. White, English novelist (1906 – 1964)

"Disobedience is the true foundation of liberty. The obedient must be slaves."

—Henry David Thoreau, American essayist, poet, and philosopher (1817 – 1862)

"A change is brought about because ordinary people do extraordinary things."

—Barack Obama, 44th President of the United States of America (b. 1961)

"Never be afraid to raise your voice for honesty and truth and compassion against injustice and lying and greed. If people all over the world . . . would do this, it would change the earth."

—William Faulkner, American novelist (1897 – 1962)

"The revolution is not an apple that falls when ripe. You have to make it fall."

—Ernesto Che Guevara, Argentine Marxist and leading figure in the Cuban Revolution (1928 – 1967)

"People have only as much liberty as they have the intelligence to want and the courage to take."

—Emma Goldman, Anarchist political activist and author (1869 – 1940)

"Whoever fights monsters should see to it that in the process he does not become a monster. And if you gaze long enough into an abyss, the abyss will gaze back into you."

—Friedrich Nietzsche, German philosopher (1844 – 1900)

👁

"The ends you serve that are selfish will take you no further than yourself but the ends you serve that are for all, in common, will take you into eternity."

—Marcus Garvey, Jamaican social activist and political leader (1887 – 1940)

👁

"If you are neutral in situations of injustice, you have chosen the side of the oppressor. If an elephant has its foot on the tail of a mouse, and you say that you are neutral, the mouse will not appreciate your neutrality."

—Desmond Tutu, South African civil rights activist (b. 1931)

👁

"No matter that patriotism is too often the refuge of scoundrels. Dissent, rebellion, and all-around hell-raising remain the true duty of patriots."

—Barbara Ehrenreich, American author and activist (b. 1941)

👁

"I was not born to be forced. I will breathe after my own fashion. Let us see who is the strongest."

—Henry David Thoreau, American essayist, poet, and philosopher (1817 – 1862)

"It's the action, not the fruit of the action, that's important. You have to do the right thing. It may not be in your power, may not be in your time, that there'll be any fruit. But that doesn't mean you stop doing the right thing. You may never know what results come from your action. But if you do nothing, there will be no result."

—Mahatma Gandhi, Indian social activist and leader of the Indian independence movement (1869 – 1948)

☉

"Let every nation know, whether it wishes us well or ill, that we shall pay any price, bear any burden, meet any hardship, support any friend, oppose any foe to assure the survival and the success of liberty."

—John F. Kennedy, 35th President of the United States of America (1917 – 1963)

☉

"To punish the oppressors of humanity is clemency; to forgive them is cruelty."

—Maximilien Robespierre, French politician and leader during the French Revolution (1758 – 1794)

☉

"He who dares not offend cannot be honest."

—Thomas Paine, American political theorist and revolutionary (1737 – 1809)

"A patriot must always be ready to defend his country against his government."

—Edward Abbey, American author and environmental activist (1927 – 1989)

○

"Tell them that the sacrifice was not in vain. Tell them that by way of the shop, the field, the skilled hand, habits of thrift and economy, by way of industrial school and college, we are coming. We are crawling up, working up, yea, bursting up. Often through oppression, unjust discrimination, and prejudice, but through them, we are coming up. And with proper habits, intelligence, and property, there is no power on earth that can permanently stay our progress."

—Booker T. Washington, American orator and civil rights activist (1856 – 1915)

○

"No real social change has ever been brought about without a revolution . . . revolution is but thought carried into action."

—Emma Goldman, Anarchist political activist and author (1869 – 1940)

○

"If modern civilisation had any meaning it was displayed in the fight against Fascism."

—Ruth McKenney, American author and journalist (1911 – 1972)

"The cure for the ills of Democracy is more Democracy."
—Jane Adams, American social activist and leader in the women's suffrage movement (1860 – 1935)

◉

"The world breaks everyone, and afterward some are strong at the broken places."
—Ernest Hemingway, American author (1899 – 1961)

◉

"There is one tradition in America I am proud to inherit. It is our first freedom and the truest expression of our Americanism: the ability to dissent without fear. It is our right to utter the words, 'I disagree.' We must feel at liberty to speak those words to our neighbors, our clergy, our educators, our news media, our lawmakers and, above all, to the one among us we elect President."
—Natalie Merchant, American singer-songwriter (b. 1963)

◉

"Rock bottom is a very good foundation to build on."
—Carl Wagner, German chemist (1901 – 1977)

◉

"Even a purely moral act that has no hope of any immediate and visible political effect can gradually and indirectly, overtime, gain in political significance."
—Vaclav Havel, Czech author and politician (1936 – 2011)

◉

"Dissent is the highest form of patriotism."
—Howard Zinn, American historian and social activist (1922 – 2010)

"The darkest places in hell are reserved for those who maintain their neutrality in times of moral crisis."

—Dante Alighieri, Italian poet (1265 – 1321)

"The enemy isn't men, or women, it's bloody stupid people and no one has the right to be stupid."

—Terry Pratchett, English novelist (1948 – 2015)

"If you wish to understand what Revolution is, call it Progress; and if you wish to understand what Progress is, call it Tomorrow."

—Victor Hugo, French novelist and poet (1802 – 1885), from *Les Misérables*

"Our whole constitutional heritage rebels at the thought of giving government the power to control men's minds."

—Thurgood Marshall, American lawyer and Associate Justice of the U. S. Supreme Court (1908 – 1993)

"The spirit of resistance to government is so valuable on certain occasions that I wish it to be always kept alive. It will often be exercised when wrong, but better so than not to be exercised at all."

—Thomas Jefferson, 3rd President of the United States of America (1743 – 1826)

"The person who has nothing for which he is willing to fight, nothing which is more important than his own personal safety, is a miserable creature and has no chance of being free unless made and kept so by the exertions of better men than himself."

—John Stuart Mill, English philosopher and political economist (1806 – 1873)

❂

"One of the chief virtues of a democracy, however, is that its defects are always visible, and under democratic processes can be pointed out and corrected."

—Harry S. Truman, 33rd President of the United States of America (1884 – 1972)

❂

"If there is no struggle, there is no progress."

—Frederick Douglass, American statesman, author, and abolitionist (1818 – 1895)

❂

"I do not fight fascists because I will win. I fight fascists because they are fascists."

—Chris Hedges, American journalist, author, and activist (b. 1956)

❂

"Fantasy. Lunacy. All revolutions are, until they happen, then they are historical inevitabilities."

—David Mitchell, English novelist (b. 1969), from *Cloud Atlas*

"In a democracy, dissent is an act of faith."

—J. William Fulbright, American politician (1905 – 1995)

◉

"Just because something bears the aspect of the inevitable one should not, therefore, go along willingly with it."

—Philip K. Dick, American science fiction author (1928 – 1982)

◉

"A riot is at bottom the language of the unheard."

—Martin Luther King, Jr., American Baptist minister and civil rights activist (1929 – 1968)

◉

"How wonderful it is that nobody need wait a single moment before starting to improve the world."

—Anne Frank, German diarist (1929 – 1945)

◉

"Every revolution was at first a thought in one man's mind."

—Ralph Waldo Emerson, American transcendentalist essayist and poet (1803 – 1882)

◉

"Sometimes we are blessed with being able to choose the time, and the arena, and the manner of our revolution, but more usually we must do battle where we are standing."

—Audre Lorde, American writer and civil rights activist (1934 – 1992)

"The highest patriotism is not a blind acceptance of official policy, but a love of one's country deep enough to call her to a higher plain."

—George McGovern, American politician (1922 – 2012)

"Repression is the seed of revolution."

—Daniel Webster, American politician and statesman (1782 – 1852)

"True patriotism hates injustice in its own land more than any-where else."

—Clarence Darrow, American lawyer and civil rights advocate (1857 – 1938)

"When principles that run against your deepest convictions begin to win the day, then battle is your calling, and peace has become sin; you must, at the price of dearest peace, lay your convictions bare before friend and enemy, with all the fire of your faith."

—Abraham Kuyper, Dutch journalist, politician, and minister (1837 – 1920)

"Anyone can become angry—that is easy. But to be angry with the right person, to the right degree, at the right time, for the right purpose, and in the right way—this is not easy."

—Aristotle, Greek philosopher (384 – 322 BC)

"I am aware that many object to the severity of my language, but is there not cause for severity? I will be as harsh as truth, and as uncompromising as justice. On this subject, I do not wish to think, or speak, or write, with moderation. No! No! Tell a man whose house is on fire to give a moderate alarm; tell him to moderately rescue his wife from the hands of the ravisher; tell the mother to gradually extricate her babe from the fire into which it has fallen;—but urge me not to use moderation in a cause like the present. I am in earnest—I will not equivocate—I will not excuse—I will not retreat a single inch—and I will be heard!"
—William Lloyd Garrison, American abolitionist and social reformer (1805 – 1879)

●

"Young women have more choices to make today about what to be. One of those choices is activist."
—Gillian Anderson, American actress (b. 1968)

●

"Activism is the rent I pay for living on the planet."
—Alice Walker, American author and poet (b. 1944)

●

"A revolution is coming—a revolution which will be peaceful if we are wise enough; compassionate if we care enough; successful if we are fortunate enough—but a revolution which is coming whether we will it or not. We can affect its character; we cannot alter its inevitability."
—Robert F. Kennedy, American politician; brother of President John F. Kennedy (1925 – 1968)

"Women are young at politics, but they are old at suffering; soon they will learn that through politics they can prevent some kinds of suffering."

—Nancy Astor, First female member of the British Parliament (1879 – 1964)

"Women had always fought for men, and for their children. Now they were ready to fight for their own human rights. Our militant movement was established."

—Emmeline Pankhurst, political activist and leader of the British suffragette movement (1858 – 1928)

"The love of one's country is a splendid thing. But why should love stop at the border?"

—Pablo Casals, Spanish cellist and conductor (1876 – 1973)

"The greatest service this country could render to the rest of the world would be to put its own house in order and to make of American civilization an example of decency, humanity, and societal success from which others could derive whatever they might find useful to their own purposes."

—George F. Kennan, American diplomat (1904 – 2005)

"Patriotism is supporting your country all the time, and your government when it deserves it."

—Mark Twain, American author and humorist (1835 – 1910)

"I consider that in no government power can be abused long. Mankind will not bear it. If a sovereign oppresses his people to a great degree, they will rise and cut off his head. There is a remedy in human nature against tyranny, that will keep us safe under every form of government."

—Samuel Johnson, English author and critic (1709 – 1784)

☉

"Man's capacity for justice makes democracy possible, but man's inclination to injustice makes democracy necessary."

—Reinhold Niebuhr, American Protestant theologian (1892 – 1971)

☉

"We must be the change we wish to see in the world."

—Mahatma Gandhi, Indian social activist and leader of the Indian independence movement (1869 – 1948)

☉

"So long as we have enough people in this country willing to fight for their rights, we'll be called a democracy."

—Roger Nash Baldwin, American activist and founder of the American Civil Liberties Union (1884 – 1981)

☉

"Rebellion to tyrants is obedience to God."

—Thomas Jefferson, 3rd President of the United States of America (1743 – 1826)

"Here in America we are descended in blood and in spirit from revolutionaries and rebels—men and women who dared to dissent from accepted doctrine. As their heirs, may we never confuse honest dissent with disloyal subversion."

—Dwight D. Eisenhower, 34th President of the United States of America (1890 – 1969)

"It is fair to assume that Parisians would not have stormed the Bastille, Gandhi would not have challenged the empire on which the sun used not to set, Martin Luther King would not have fought white supremacy in 'the land of the free and the home of the brave,' without their sense of manifest injustices that could be overcome. They were not trying to achieve a perfectly just world (even if there were any agreement on what that would be like), but they did want to remove clear injustices to the extent they could."

—Amartya Sen, Economist and philosopher (b. 1933)

"You cannot buy the revolution. You cannot make the revolution. You can only be the revolution. It is in your spirit, or it is nowhere."

—Ursula K. Le Guin, American novelist (b. 1929), from *The Dispossessed*

"Our masters have not heard the people's voice for generations and it is much, much louder than they care to remember."

—Alan Moore, American writer and comic book author (b. 1953), from *V for Vendetta*

◉

"There comes a time when the cup of endurance runs over, and men are no longer willing to be plunged into an abyss of injustice where they experience the blackness of corroding despair."

—Martin Luther King, Jr., American Baptist minister and civil rights activist (1929 – 1968)

◉

"We beg no longer; we entreat no more; we petition no more. We defy them."

—William Jennings Bryan, American politician (1860 – 1925)

◉

"America did not invent human rights. In a very real sense, it is the other way round. Human rights invented America."

—Jimmy Carter, 39th President of the United States of America (b. 1924)

◉

"The only way to support a revolution is to make your own."

—Abbie Hoffman, political and social activist (1936 – 1989)

"One ought not to be obstinate, except when one ought to be; but when one ought to be, then one ought to be unshakable."
—Charles Maurice de Talleyrand-Périgord, French politician and diplomat (1754 – 1838)

◉

"Thought that is silenced is always rebellious. Majorities, of course, are often mistaken. This is why the silencing of minorities is necessarily dangerous. Criticism and dissent are the indispensable antidote to major delusions."
—Alan Barth, American journalist (1906 – 1979)

◉

"Unless someone like you cares a whole awful lot, Nothing is going to get better. It's not."
—Dr. Seuss, American children's book author and illustrator (1904 – 1991), from *The Lorax*

◉

"Revolution is not the uprising against pre-existing order, but the setting-up of a new order contradictory to the traditional one."
—José Ortega y Gasset, Spanish philosopher and essayist (1883 – 1955)

◉

"Under conditions of tyranny it is far easier to act than to think."
—Hannah Arendt, German-American political theorist (1906 – 1975)

"Persuasion, perseverance and patience are the best advocates on questions depending on the will of others."

—Thomas Jefferson, 3rd President of the United States of America (1743 – 1826)

"There is absolutely no greater high than challenging the power structure as a nobody, giving it your all, and winning. I think I've learned that lesson twice now. The essence of successful revolution, be it for an individual, a community of individuals, or a nation, depends on accepting that challenge."

—Abbie Hoffman, political and social activist (1936 – 1989)

"Whether in chains or in laurels, liberty knows nothing but victories."

—Wendell Phillips, American attorney and activist (1811 – 1884)

"The activist is not the man who says the river is dirty. The activist is the man who cleans up the river."

—Ross Perot, American politician (b. 1930)

"The arc of a moral universe is long, but it bends toward justice."

—Martin Luther King, Jr., American Baptist minister and civil rights activist (1929 – 1968)

"Those who make peaceful revolution impossible will make violent revolution inevitable."

—John F. Kennedy, 35th President of the United States of America (1917 – 1963)

◉

"There is nothing wrong with America that cannot be cured with what is right in America."

—William Jefferson Clinton, 42nd President of the United States of America (b. 1946)

◉

"Freedom is an indivisible word. If we want to enjoy it, and fight for it, we must be prepared to extend it to everyone, whether they are rich or poor, whether they agree with us or not, no matter what their race or the colour of their skin."

—Wendell Lewis Willkie, American lawyer and politician (1892 – 1944)